"I won't leave

"Yes, you will."

Gripping his face with both hands, Summer shook her head. "Don't go after him. He'll kill you."

"I can't let him get away, only to have another chance to try again."

She pressed her forehead to his, heart throbbing. "We have to go together."

"There's no time for this." Pulling away, he snatched her wrist and yanked her upright.

She lurched to her feet.

He grabbed her purse from the nightstand and shoved it toward her. "He's rigging the house to blow." His voice was a harsh whisper. "You have to get out."

Panic flared along with an icy jolt of fear. She shook her head again. How could he ask her to leave him behind?

Logan curled his hand in her hair, leaned in and dipped his head down. "Please," he said through gritted teeth. "Listen to me."

Then his mouth crushed against hers in a kiss that shocked the hell out of her.

CORRALLED IN CUTTHROAT CREEK

JUNO RUSHDAN

INTRIGUE

To the heroes who may not know where they fit in, but who are never afraid to stand up for justice.

Harlequin®
INTRIGUE™

ISBN-13: 978-1-335-45735-6

Corralled in Cutthroat Creek

Copyright © 2025 by Juno Rushdan

 Harlequin Enterprises ULC
22 Adelaide St. West, 41st Floor
Toronto, Ontario M5H 4E3, Canada
www.Harlequin.com

Printed in Lithuania

MIX
Paper | Supporting
responsible forestry
FSC® C021394

Juno Rushdan is a veteran US Air Force intelligence officer and award-winning author. Her books are action-packed and fast-paced. Critics from *Kirkus Reviews* and *Library Journal* have called her work "heart-pounding James Bond–ian adventure" that "will captivate lovers of romantic thrillers." For a free book, visit her website: www.junorushdan.com.

Books by Juno Rushdan

Harlequin Intrigue

Cowboy State Lawmen: Duty and Honor

Wyoming Mountain Investigation
Wyoming Ranch Justice
Wyoming Undercover Escape
Wyoming Christmas Conspiracy
Wyoming Double Jeopardy
Corralled in Cutthroat Creek

Cowboy State Lawmen

Wyoming Winter Rescue
Wyoming Christmas Stalker
Wyoming Mountain Hostage
Wyoming Mountain Murder
Wyoming Cowboy Undercover
Wyoming Mountain Cold Case

Fugitive Heroes: Topaz Unit

Rogue Christmas Operation
Alaskan Christmas Escape
Disavowed in Wyoming
An Operative's Last Stand

Visit the Author Profile page at Harlequin.com.

CAST OF CHARACTERS

Logan Powell—A part-time rancher and full-time special agent with the Wyoming Justice Department Division of Criminal Investigation. This cowboy is eager for a second chance to cozy up to Summer Stratton, but investigating the death of his cousin leads him down an unexpected and dangerous path.

Summer Stratton—A brilliant, young lawyer who refuses to be intimidated or scared off. She'll stop at nothing to find the truth despite the risks involved, but the last thing she expected was for the death of her best friend to bring her face-to-face with the one man she's never been able to forget.

Chance Reyes—He's a sharp attorney in charge of the Ironside Protection Services (IPS) office in Big Sky Country. He also grew up with Logan and won't hesitate to help him.

Vern Tofteland—Unaccustomed to being challenged, this sheriff has little patience for Summer and Logan. He'll do almost anything to get them out of town, but would he break the law?

Bo Lennox—IPS agent.

Declan Hart—A special investigator with Montana DCI.

Tak Yazzie—IPS agent.

Eli Easton—IPS agent.

Chapter One

Her gut twisted. She wasn't alone. Someone else was in the house.

More floorboards creaked somewhere downstairs.

Summer Stratton couldn't tell exactly which room the sound had come from since she wasn't very familiar with the place, only having been inside it on a handful of occasions. The house belonged to her longtime best friend, Dani Granger, who was now deceased.

Murdered.

Summer refused to believe that Dani's death had been a convenient accident.

Was the killer the same person creeping around now?

In the upstairs primary bedroom, Summer stared at the box under the bed. Checking the contents would have to wait. Switching off the heavy black flashlight, she stood up and stilled. The only thing sparing her from being plunged into total darkness was the moonlight filtering in through the parted curtains of one window.

Something crashed downstairs in the back part of the house, making her jump. Whatever it was had been big and heavy. Must've been knocked over. Possibly in the kitchen.

Then silence.

Despite the July heat trapped in the house, cold sweat trickled down her spine.

Wind hissed through the old house, causing its bones to rattle and squeak. Branches from the trees around the place clattered, scraping against the siding. A storm was gathering. The massive evergreen close to the window stood like an ominous sentry in the shadows.

She had hoped to find what she was searching for, sneak out and make it back to the small cabin she'd rented on the outskirts of Cutthroat Creek before the rain started and without being discovered.

Two fails.

But could this one misstep cost her life?

A thump echoed in tandem with a screech downstairs. Glass or porcelain shattered. Maybe the intruder had bumped into something. Had the noise come from the living room?

That was the one space in the house crammed with tchotchkes and collectibles on every surface like mini booby traps.

The noises had started in the kitchen and were now coming from the living room, she supposed. He was working his way through the house, from back to front.

She wasn't sure if she should move and try to hide. The old floorboards might give away her position.

Rain pitter-pattered on the roof. Pulses of lightning flashed outside, illuminating fat beads of rain quivering down the windowpanes. The wind picked up, rustling the branches, and the mixture of noises made it hard for her to pinpoint the location of the footsteps in the house.

Thunder cracked. The rumble was in the distance, shifting closer. As the sound faded outside, another one rose inside—the groan of the stairs.

A shiver scuttled over her body like a legion of icy spiders. *He's coming up.*

Summer glanced around the bedroom for her purse that had her pepper spray. She never left home in Seattle without a canister of Mace and had been sure to pack several in her bags, even putting one on her key chain during the seven-hour drive from Washington to Montana.

No handbag in sight. She swore to herself as she remembered where she'd left it.

Her purse was downstairs. With her Mace. On the coffee table in the living room. Right along with her cell phone and the keys to her car that she'd hidden in the woods.

Another slow creak from the weight ascending on the risers set her pulse pounding.

The man creeping up the stairs stood between her and all possibility of calling for help and getting rescued. Between her and the sole weapon she'd brought to defend herself. Between her and freedom—the only way to escape.

Standing there, she was rooted in place by fear, with a virtual bull's-eye on her forehead. The guy in the house could be there to simply scare her away, give her a more forceful warning.

But deep down she suspected that was wishful thinking. The reality was she'd already been warned. Several times.

Anything could happen to her out here. *He* could do anything to her. Hurt her, or worse.

Kill her.

She shook her head, needing to calm down and think clearly. Shuffling around in haste and leading him straight to her wasn't a much better option either. She strategized, planned, thought things through ad nauseam.

Rushing always led to a regrettable choice.

Lightning flashed again. Within seconds, there would be thunder. That was when she'd hide. Hopefully, the noise would be enough to mask the sound of her movements.

Summer waited. The storm was drawing nearer. Thunder would come sooner than the last time.

Down the hallway, a door squeaked open. He was up on the second floor.

A boom bellowed loud enough to rattle the windows.

Summer gave in to the flight response flooding her system and dashed across the room on the balls of her feet to the back wall, where there were two closets. She chose the second one, closest to the windows, farthest from the door, and ducked inside, shutting it as quickly and quietly as possible.

The primary bedroom was the last one at the far end of the hall. Eventually, whoever was skulking around inside the house, searching for her, would make their way down there and find her.

Then what?

Panic flared hot. She felt around gingerly, frantically, for a baseball bat. A golf club. A shotgun—not that she knew how to use one. Something she could use to protect herself, doing her best not to knock anything over by accident. Only clothes and hangers in the closet.

No weapon within easy reach. Her heart sank.

She'd been warned to stay away, to stop poking her nose where it didn't belong, to go back home to Seattle. Better to be safe than sorry. That was what she'd been told.

The house was being watched or she was. Either was bad. But it was undeniably clear that one, most likely both, were under surveillance.

Going to the Granger house late at night, under the cover of darkness when she'd normally be asleep, had seemed like a good idea. Until now.

Breathe. Think. Going off the deep end isn't going to do you any good.

No help was coming. She hadn't told anybody that she was going to the house tonight. Not her sisters or her parents. None of them lived in Montana. It wasn't as though they could run over in the nick of time even if she had her cell phone to call them. Or 911. Not that a call to the local authorities would go well, because technically, the sheriff would consider her a trespasser.

There weren't even any neighbors within screaming distance for her go to, provided she could get out of the house. In fact, the closest one was a couple of miles down the road.

Her stomach lurched as the hopelessness of her predicament set in. She was all alone in the middle of nowhere, with someone in the house who wanted her to stop investigating.

Dani had already been silenced. Maybe this time the murderer wouldn't hesitate to kill her, too.

Tightening her sweaty grip on her Maglite, she tamped down her despair. She needed to think of a way out of this. Alive and hopefully unharmed. Clutching the flashlight to her chest, she clenched her fingers around it. The long handle was thick and heavy-duty and might suffice as a makeshift weapon in a pinch. She was certainly in a sticky situation. One she intended to survive.

This was costing her everything. Summer was on the brink of losing her dream job with a top law firm and possibly her life, all for the sake of exposing the truth and for justice. For Dani.

She took a deep breath and forced herself to focus.

Get out of the house by any means necessary. Grab keys. Mace. Run to the car.

That was the plan, albeit a flimsy one, but it would have to do.

Floorboards near the bedroom groaned. Heavy footfalls

entered the room and stopped. Adrenaline swamped her, and she struggled to listen through the roar of her drumming pulse in her ears.

A jarring screech made her flinch. Sounded like he moved something. The bed? She covered her mouth with a hand to keep from screaming.

Footsteps crossed the room. Toward the corner, on the other end of the wall. Hinges squeaked as a door opened. Hangers scraped on the metal rod. He was checking the closet.

A cold tightness threaded through her sternum while a greasy sliding sensation took hold in her stomach. He would move on to the next closet and find her. Impossible to hide.

Fight and run. Stick to the plan.

Thunder roared overhead, making the house shudder, the loud booms resonating in her bones. Through the fading rumble, the sound of footsteps thudding across the hardwood carried. Each one drawing nearer. Steadily. Slowly.

The walls closed in. Her stomach roiled.

Oh, God. She could do this. Had to. No other choice.

Summer braced herself, holding the flashlight tight, and prepared to attack whoever was on the other side of the door.

The heavy footsteps edged closer, approaching the closet, and stopped in front of the door. A dense knot swelled in her throat. Hands shaking, she tasted acid fear on her tongue.

The doorknob twisted with a creak.

She shoved on the door with all her might before he fully opened it as a cry cracked loose from inside her. The surprising force jostled the person back. Then she saw him. A man wearing a ski mask.

Summer swung the flashlight, hitting him in the head. She kicked him, going for the groin. The guy doubled over with a grunt and cursed her. She swung the Maglite again, whacking the back of his skull and knocking him to the ground. She didn't waste a second. Whirling around, she bolted for the door. Dashed from the bedroom.

Bang! A blast of gunfire split the air, the deafening sound chilling her to the bone.

Was she hit? She wasn't sure but didn't stop running.

It took a second to register that she didn't feel any pain. She kept moving. Down the hall. To the stairwell.

Summer grabbed the railing and hit the steps as another shot exploded, the bullet striking the wall, bits of plaster erupting with debris hitting her face. Screaming, she hunched and instinctively covered the back of her head with the hand that held the flashlight.

She might not be so lucky if he fired again.

Footsteps pounded after her, closing the distance between them. The terrifying sound made her stomach clench and bile burn her throat. Could she make it? She didn't stop racing down the steps, one hand gripping the rail to prevent her from tumbling down face-first. Adrenaline pumped hot in her veins. She was almost at the bottom of the stairwell.

Then came two more blasts.

And her luck ran out as searing pain slashed through her.

LOGAN POWELL HAD pulled his truck up in front of his cousin's house and cut the engine when he heard the unmistakable sound.

Gunfire!

Even through the rain and the low music in the cab of the truck, he was certain it had been a gun's report and not a clap of thunder.

But no one was supposed to be in the house. His cousin Dani was dead, as well as her parents. Her next of kin was their uncle, Ric Granger, who was back home in Wyoming, and Dani's friend Summer Stratton was staying in a place she'd rented near town.

He jumped out of the truck into the pouring rain so fast he didn't take the usual precautions of calling 911 first. Drawing his service weapon from the holster on his hip beside his badge, he charged toward the porch, getting soaked.

Bang. Bang.

In the quick muzzle flashes that lit up the darkness inside the house, he spotted someone running from the bottom of the landing, being chased by another person barreling down the stairs.

Logan stormed up the porch, his steps soft and stealthy, and almost kicked the door inward. But he had the element of surprise to his advantage and didn't want to give it up unless necessary. He tried the doorknob. It turned. Unlocked. With his Glock at the ready, he swept inside the house.

Noises of a violent struggle came from the living room— grunting and panicked screams, flesh being hit, items clattering to the floor. He hurried deeper inside, glancing at the stairway and noting bullet holes in the wall, and rounded the corner into the living room.

A guy dressed in all black with a ski mask covering his face grabbed a woman from behind and yanked her around. The woman was fighting back. She stomped on the guy's foot and threw an elbow into his gut. The guy swore, hurling threats, but didn't let her go.

The two were locked in a deadly tussle. Logan didn't have a clear shot—no way to guarantee he didn't hit her by accident. He holstered his gun and charged forward, his boots crunching on broken porcelain.

The assailant whirled at the sudden noise, letting the woman go.

Logan tackled the gunman and rammed him hard enough to send them crashing to the floor, but the woman fell with them. Her legs were caught beneath them as they fought.

Blow for blow was exchanged. Needing to prevent the other guy from shooting him, Logan kept the masked man's wrist holding the gun locked in a tight grip. Still, Logan took a solid hook to the jaw and tasted blood, but he didn't pay attention to the pain since he was more focused on delivering his own. He managed to grab the guy by his shirt and yank him to the side.

Free, the woman scrambled up from the floor. She was panting, her dark hair wild, scanning the room as though she was looking for something. He caught a glimpse of her face.

Summer?

He'd met her once, years ago, but couldn't be sure it was her in the dim light and the frenzy of the attack.

Logan threw a knee in the masked man's stomach and punched him in the face while the woman scooped something up from the table and dashed toward the kitchen. They wrestled, the two of them both trying to climb to their feet. The assailant smashed his head into Logan's face, nearly breaking his nose. The blow left him reeling. His hand loosened on the man's wrist, and he reached out to steady himself. The edge of something bit into his palm.

A glint of silver flashed in the moonlight as the masked man raised the gun.

Logan wrapped his fingers around the object his hand had found—a long, broken shard—and swung it around, stabbing the man in his wrist.

Howling in the pain, the guy staggered back, but didn't drop the gun on reflex. He lashed out with the pistol, giving Logan a sharp rap across the head with the weapon.

Stunned, Logan dropped to a knee and pulled his Glock at almost the same time.

In a blur, the masked man spun and ran for the front door. His footsteps pounded down the steps, the sound fading beneath the rain.

Logan swallowed blood and stood with a groan. For a second, he worried that the woman had fled out through the back door and might run into whoever had attacked her. He hurried through the dark house to the kitchen.

The refrigerator had been knocked over. With the top resting on the edge of one of the counters, the fridge blocked the back door. She was up on top of the counter, prying open the window above the sink.

"Hey," Logan said, hurrying up behind her, and touched her arm. "Are you hu—"

She kicked back, throwing a foot in his gut and whirled, her right hand raised.

Logan registered the can of pepper spray in her grasp. Too late.

The blast of stinging mist him in the eyes and nose. "Oww!" Flinging his hands up, he ducked away, trying to avoid the worst of the spray. Still, some got into his open mouth. Gasping for clean air, he couldn't haul in enough. He stumbled backward, his stomach heaving. Through the burning that blinded him, he yelled, "Stop." Sucking another sharp breath at the combination of his stinging eyes and his skin on fire, he coughed and choked. "I'm a cop."

Chapter Two

A cop?

Summer stared at him in disbelief. "Prove it." With a trembling hand, she kept the pepper spray pointed at the stranger's face.

The man gagged and coughed, trying to catch his breath. He unhooked a badge from his waistband and held it up.

She climbed down from the counter and winced from the pain in her arm. The bullet had grazed her shoulder, leaving a bloody, sore mess, but she was thankful the injury wasn't serious. Cautiously, she approached him, and took his badge for closer inspection. Looked real enough.

Special agent with the Wyoming Division of Criminal Investigation.

He *was* a cop, but that didn't automatically make him a good guy. Not in this town. "Now prove you don't want to hurt me." The last time she came to the house, the sheriff had *coincidentally* showed up shortly thereafter—as though someone had called him, or he'd been the one following her—and intimidated her.

Best to leave well enough alone. It's better to be safe than sorry, the sheriff had told her right before he threatened to arrest her for trespassing, insisted she hightail it out of town and go back to Washington.

"What?" With his head lowered, he wiped his eyes and

coughed like he was hacking up a lung. "Why would I hurt you? I just saved you from that guy."

True, but she'd learned you couldn't be too careful. "What are you doing in this house? Who are you?"

"This is my family's house. I'm Logan Powell. Dani Granger's cousin."

"Oh my gosh. I thought you were..." Summer stepped closer, putting the pepper spray away inside her cross-body purse. "Sorry. I didn't realize."

Once she had learned about Dani's death, she'd flown out to Cutthroat Creek. She'd missed the funeral, but she had a chance to talk to Dani's closest living relative, her uncle, Ric Granger. He happened to still be in town, deciding what to do with the property. She'd convinced him that Dani had been murdered and asked him to hold off on selling. Ric had promised to send someone to help her investigate, possibly his son, Matt Granger, a cop whom she'd met previously. He hadn't mentioned when someone might show up or that someone else might come in Matt's stead. Much less that it would be Logan Powell.

"A little help over here," he said. "Where's the sink? I need to rinse the pepper spray out of my eyes."

His eyes were watering, and his nose didn't look too good either. He took a half-blind step toward her.

"We should get out of the kitchen." Pepper spray lingered in the air, irritating her eyes and throat as well, simply from being in the area. Taking him by the arm, she led him from the kitchen.

The living room was in shambles. Many of the trinkets and collectibles, items she'd consider to be dust collectors, were in pieces, scattered on the floor. At least Ric Granger wasn't attached to anything in the house and had been uncertain what to do with everything.

"I'm so sorry," she said. "I was terrified." She guided him through the living room and to the stairs since there wasn't a powder room on the first floor. "I thought the other man might kill me. Then you came up behind me and I panicked." She put his hand on the railing and kept her palm on his arm. "It's dark and I had no idea who you were or why you were there. Whether you'd attack me, too." And in the dim light from the window, his muscular shadow was more than a little frightening.

"I get it. Totally understandable." His tone was gentle when she wouldn't have blamed him for being irate. "I just need some water so I can rinse my eyes out."

Picking up the pace, she led him to the hallway bathroom, the second door on the left, and flicked on the light. "Thanks for taking this so well."

"Sink?"

"Oh, right." She steered him to the sink and turned on the spigot. "Sorry," she apologized for a third time, feeling awful for hurting him by accident.

He bent over and splashed handfuls of water onto his face again and again, rinsing out the Mace from his eyes and nose. Another palmful he scooped into his mouth, swished it around and spit.

In addition to the chemicals, blood hit the sink. She guessed it was from the fight in the living room. Several times more he repeated the process.

Summer sagged with a mix of shame and embarrassment. Her nerves were on edge. It was hard to tell who the good guys were anymore. Guilt prickled her for being the cause of his hissing gasps of discomfort. She put a hand on his back, not knowing what else to do to help him. His taut muscles flexed under his drenched T-shirt and in his exposed, sinewed arms.

The sheer strength of his body took her breath away. He was ripped.

Logan shut off the water and stood upright. He was six feet easily, maybe an inch or so taller. Curly dark blond hair glistened like gold in the bathroom light. And he was built like a freaking Viking.

Or maybe she had been watching way too much of the History channel.

Tearing her gaze from him, she looked for a towel. She went to the linen closet, grabbed a hand towel and gave it to him.

"Thanks." Wiping his face, he trudged over to the bathtub and plopped down on the edge.

She sat beside him. "You should've told me who you were instead of creeping up behind me like that." The situation had demanded that she act first and ask questions later.

"The guy who attacked you fled out the front door," he said. "I was worried you might run into him outside. Figured I'd make sure you were all right and stayed safe before I bothered with an introduction."

"Oh." That made sense, which in turn made her feel even worse. Not only had he saved her, but he'd been worried about her safety. "Sorry I nailed you with my Mace."

"No need to apologize. Again." He blinked rapidly. "You were scared and didn't know who I was."

Why did he have to be so nice about it? His kindness only compounded her guilt.

"Let me get you a bath towel," she said, rising to her feet. "You're soaked through." Not only was he drenched from the rain, but she was certain his shirt had absorbed a good deal of the pepper spray. The chemicals would continue to bother him.

She hurried back to the closet and pulled out a large, fluffy beige towel for him to drape around himself.

Turning around, she staggered to a halt as he grabbed the bottom of his T-shirt and hauled the wet top over his head.

Her jaw dropped, and she gaped at him, at all that exposed, tanned skin. At his bulging pecs. At his rippling abs. At his long, lean legs that were clad in wet denim. He wasn't overly bulky with muscle. Lean and sculpted. A well-honed physique too impressive to ignore, though she tried and failed.

"Wow," she breathed. Smart, good-looking men with an athletic build were her type. Add in chivalrous and she'd never encountered such an alluring combination.

"Huh?" He raised his head and looked up at her, squinting red, irritated eyes.

"Um, nothing." But he was definitely something. Unexpected in more ways than one.

"My vision is still blurry," he said. "Those sprays are oil-based. Hard to get off. Can you grab some soap for me?"

She slung the towel over her good shoulder and picked up a container of oat milk bodywash from the side of the tub. Turning on the bathtub faucet, she passed him the soap. He leaned over, washed his face twice and rinsed it thoroughly before taking the towel from her. She sat back down beside him.

He dried his face and ran the towel through his hair. "That's better. Let's try the introduction one more time. Logan Powell." He proffered his hand as he wiped his eyes.

His grip was strong and steady, his palm warm.

"Summer Stratton. We met a few years back when Dani's mother passed away." She had died suddenly from heart disease. The death had devastated Dani, and Summer had done everything possible to lighten the load for her friend and Dani's dad, who had been heartbroken. After the funeral, once exhaustion set in, she and Logan had shared a quiet moment alone together on the back porch. She'd sipped a glass of wine while he nursed a beer. Chatted in a way that she never had before with a man—open and vulnerable, simply herself.

"I wasn't sure if you'd remember me," he said. "It was so long ago. I didn't want to presume and be wrong."

"You're hard to forget." Rare to find a man who had all the four *C*'s. Confident. Capable. Cute *and* considerate.

He'd been easy to talk to, things flowing naturally between them. In the crowd of strangers who'd come by to pay their respects, Summer had felt like an outsider. Until that moment alone with Logan. The two of them had been in a calm bubble out on the back porch, a little haven where she felt like she was home.

She'd wished he'd asked for her number. But what kind of man picked up a woman at a funeral?

Besides, her life was in Washington and his in Wyoming.

"I could say the same about you," he said. "The way you took charge, organizing and handling things from the flowers to the food. Dealing with problems without making a fuss. Impressive." Logan draped the towel on the side of the tub. "Wish we were meeting again under better circumstances, Ms. Stratton." Shifting in her direction, he looked at her. No more squinting. Direct gaze.

Piercing eyes so blue they were simply stunning met hers and then he smiled. Even those dimples were unforgettable.

Oh, my.

Chapter Three

A surge of intense awareness struck Logan like lightning as he stared at the brown-skinned beauty. Her face was stunningly familiar despite the fact that it had been several years, five to be exact, since he'd last seen her. As if he'd spent the brief time that they had been together memorizing each feature.

An oddly disturbing thought. Still, he continued to stare at her. Luminous, dark almond-shaped eyes. Smooth complexion. Lush, full lips. Her shoulder-length hair was tousled and wild, yet sexy with bouncy curls.

Why did death keep bringing him back together with this gorgeous woman?

"Please don't call me Ms. Stratton. It makes me feel like I'm at work. Summer is fine. My dad calls me Sunshine, but that makes me feel as though I'm eight years old instead of twenty-eight."

"I like Summer. As a season," he said, thinking of the first swim of the year in the lake, the busiest time on the ranch, the big Fourth of July celebration his family always hosted, his birthday and ideal weather, "and also as a name. It's beautiful." Like her.

"Thanks."

Blood on her shoulder caught his eye. It had soaked

through the sleeve of her top and was dripping down her arm. "You're hurt."

This entire time she was tending to him, making sure that he was all right while she was injured. Bleeding. A wound she no doubt sustained because of the man he'd fought off. Anger rose and he tried hard to control his temper but seeing her hurt… Knowing that man had been the one to harm her. And for Summer to ignore the pain and focus solely on him with no thought of herself had Logan gritting his teeth.

"Why didn't you say anything?" he asked and reached for her.

But she cringed, making him lower his hand.

"It slipped my mind after I pepper-sprayed you," she said. "I was a little preoccupied worrying about your eyes and hoping I didn't blind you."

"What happened?" He gestured to her arm.

"That guy shot me. I was lucky. He nearly took my head off. I think a bullet only nicked me."

"Any idea who he was?"

"No," she said and glanced at her shoulder. "It hurts like the dickens."

"Thought it slipped your mind."

"Well, you've brought it back to the forefront, and now I know you're going to be okay."

His face stung, and would for a while, but he was fine. She was the one in need of medical attention. "Permission to touch you, so I can take a look?" he asked.

She nodded. "I don't mind you touching me."

Their gazes locked and silence fell. A pleasant moment of quiet brought another pop of awareness—a gut punch— something so hard-hitting it took the air out of his lungs and weakened his knees.

Summer shook her head and quickly added, "I was nervous about the pain when you reached for me. I have a low tolerance for it. Never dealt well with physical discomfort."

Moving from the tub, he dropped to a knee on the other side of her where he could see the wound better. "I'll go slowly. If it hurts too much just let me know." He grabbed the hem of her short sleeve shirt and peeled it up. She winced, but didn't complain. "A lot deeper than a nick. But it passed right through. I can clean and bandage it for you, but you're going to need stitches. Otherwise, it'll leave a nasty scar."

Summer sighed. "I hate hospitals and with a gunshot wound they're going to call the sheriff."

"You say that like it's a bad thing." He got up and opened the cabinet under the sink. A medical kit peeked out from behind a stack of toilet paper, and he grabbed it.

"The sheriff hasn't been too helpful. In fact, I'd say he's been the opposite."

Law enforcement officers tended to get territorial and didn't appreciate civilians meddling in their investigations. Despite their good intentions, private citizens sometimes mucked things up or put themselves in harm's way. At the moment, he was inclined to place Summer in the latter category.

"We need to report what happened earlier anyway," he said. "Do you think the guy who attacked you was a burglar?" Cutthroat Creek had a few affluent areas. This wasn't one of them. Mostly farmland with owners making ends meet. Yet something had provoked the guy to break in wearing a mask and gloves and to carry gun. "Or was there more to it?"

"He wasn't a burglar," she said with such conviction that

it was hard not to believe her. "He was here to stop me from nosing around by scaring me or…killing me."

His protective instincts flared hot again. "Once shots are fired, things have escalated beyond a scare tactic."

"Either way, the sheriff won't do anything about it. I don't know if he's being paid off or if he just thinks I'm delusional about what happened to Dani."

Logan sat beside her, where he could easily tend to her bloody shoulder. "I came up for her funeral with my uncle Ric and his son, Matt." Not only had he wanted to support Matt, but he had also been confident Summer would be there to say goodbye to her friend. Surprise, surprise, she had been a no-show. "The sheriff told my uncle and Matt that Dani was drunk and crashed into a tree." Logan had gone to get groceries while they went to the sheriff's office. Based on everything he'd heard, the circumstances were tragic but had appeared straightforward to him. Uncle Ric had stayed behind, trying to decide what to do with the property. Finally, he'd returned to Wyoming under the impression that Dani might have been murdered. His uncle had insisted someone with a badge needed to go to Cutthroat Creek to help Dani's friend, a lawyer, investigate and discover the truth. "I take it you don't think that's what really happened."

"No, I don't."

He opened the med kit. Took out gauze and saline solution. "Mind sharing your theory?"

"How well did you know Dani or about how much trouble she was having out here?"

Dani was only a cousin through marriage and with her living in another state, there wasn't much cause for them to be close. "I've only been here a couple of times." Every instance had been to keep Matt company. Logan and his brothers had grown up alongside Matt, thought of him as a brother for all intents and purposes. When they were younger, Matt had a hard time fitting in, feeling as though he didn't belong anywhere. Logan did what he could to show him family would stand by him through anything. "Honestly, I didn't know her well at all." Wiping the blood from her arm, he worked his way up toward her shoulder. "As for the trouble she was having, I heard she lost her father last year." Uncle Ric's brother had passed from cancer. Work had prevented Logan from attending the funeral. "Things weren't going well on the farm, and she was having financial difficulty. Something to do with a problem with her cattle." He squirted saline solution in the wound, and she flinched. "Sorry."

"It's okay." Her gaze lifted to his, her brown eyes glowing with a softness. "I kind of deserved it for Macing you."

Logan grinned. Not that getting pepper-sprayed in the face was a joking matter. Her tone was so apologetic, her eyes so full of remorse—she was sweet, for a lawyer—that he wanted to make her feel better. Simply couldn't help it.

For a second, he was awed by the realization that he couldn't shake the bizarre feeling of connection to this woman. It had been the same way five years ago. There'd been the preparations, a wake, the funeral. And through it all, Summer had been at Dani's side. Then at the repast later at the house, they'd stood out on the back porch talking. He'd been mesmerized by her. Warm and charming and completely at ease with herself. Even after he'd returned home to Wyoming, the young, whip-smart attorney had stayed on his mind.

"Ric told me Matt might come up to investigate," she

said. "He didn't mention the possibility of anyone else. I'd say this was a nice surprise, but…" Her voice trailed off.

No need for her to finish the sentence.

He wrapped gauze around the wound, bandaging it. The best that could be done until she got stitches.

"Matt is on vacation with his fiancée. He's had it planned for a while and didn't want to cancel," Logan said. Matt and Hannah weren't the types to take downtime often. No one in his family was. Workaholics the lot of them. Logan wanted the two lovebirds to get away, unwind, and have some fun for once instead of working their *day jobs*—a relative term since both Matt and Hannah were cops—while also putting in time on the ranch. "My brother Jackson, he's a US marshal, wanted to do it. He actually lives nearby but he's traveling right now on a fugitive recovery assignment. Uncle Ric felt the situation was urgent and couldn't wait. So, I stepped up and volunteered."

Everyone else was busy these days. Falling in love. Getting married. Having babies. Everyone except for him and his youngest brother, the marshal. They all joked that Jackson was the forgotten one. Left home as soon as he turned eighteen and just visited for a special occasion—wedding, christening or funeral. Only their mother kept track of him with regular phone calls. In many ways, Logan admired how his little brother had forged a path apart from their family, away from home, outside of Wyoming. Heck, Logan still lived on the ranch, along with his brothers Monty and Holden, and his cousin Matt. His other brother, Sawyer, only left last year after love led him to Virginia. The ranch had been Logan's home all his life. One day he'd leave, if he ever found the right reason.

"I've met Jackson," she said, slight hesitation in her voice. "We both attended the funeral for Dani's father last year. Your brother, he's not…" her lips flattened in a tight line, like she was choosing her words carefully "…a people person. Not like you. I don't think he would've been quite so understanding about the pepper spray."

"Jackson can be standoffish with strangers." Downright cold and curt, to be honest. "He doesn't have the Powell family charm." What his brother lacked in people skills, he made up for with fierce loyalty and ferocious tenacity. Once he fought for a cause or a person, he didn't back down. No one ever said that Jackson Powell didn't have determination.

"It's generous of you to take time off and come out to investigate on behalf of a cousin you barely knew."

If only his reasons had been entirely selfless. His ulterior motive had been to see Summer Stratton again. This time he knew for certain that she'd be in Cutthroat Creek. Logan's interest in her had been stirred from the moment they were introduced, and had intensified during the events surrounding the funeral. Still, he'd realized there was a possibility he would be disappointed when he came back here.

People changed, sometimes drastically over five years, and were often different at funerals than their usual, day-to-day selves.

Not Summer. She was the same genuine, kindhearted woman he remembered.

But he was unable to admit his selfish cause for being in Cutthroat. He stayed quiet, letting her believe he was a better man than he really was.

"You and your uncle Ric must be close."

"Not really," Logan said, sadly. The distance between them had been entirely his uncle's choice. "Uncle Ric helps manage the Shooting Star-Longhorn Ranch at home, but he acts more like an employee than family."

"Why is that?"

Logan shrugged. "The situation is complicated. I'll tell you another time. Let's just say coming out here was the right thing to do. I might not have known Dani well, but if her death wasn't an accident, she deserves justice and my uncle needs peace of mind. Figured I'd put some of the leave days I've got banked to good use. Only problem is I'm not really sure what I'm here to investigate."

The sheriff's office had closed the case. Logan didn't have the faintest idea why his uncle and Summer thought it should be reopened beyond a hunch.

"Dani was my best friend," Summer said.

Logan recalled that they had gone to college together and had been roommates throughout all their undergrad years, starting on campus and eventually sharing an apartment close to the school.

"We always stayed in touch, talking several times a month," she continued. "A couple of years ago, she contacted me with suspicions that her cattle were being poisoned."

"By whom?"

"Einhorn Industries. They own the paper mill and waste recycling plant in town. Einhorn manufactures fertilizer from biosolids. They claim it's safe, but it isn't. Dani discovered it was making her cattle sick and convinced her father not to buy it anymore."

"Did it make a difference when they stopped using it?"

"Unfortunately, no. Einhorn has a facility not far from here. Dani suspected the chemicals from the biosolids were polluting the creek that not only runs through this property but is also adjacent to the waste recycling plant. At my firm in Seattle, I've helped work on class action lawsuits against companies like Einhorn as an associate. I told her how to go about collecting evidence to see if there was a possible case. She found four other farmers having similar problems. I helped convince them to become plaintiffs as well. We were getting close to nailing Einhorn. We had almost everything we needed. Then I found out Dani was dead."

"The timing is a bit suspicious, granted, but her blood alcohol was 0.3." For a woman Dani's size, that was dangerously high and could've been enough to kill her even if she hadn't gotten behind the wheel of a car. "She shouldn't have been driving the night of her accident." The only positive thing was that nobody else had been killed. Way too often it seemed that passengers or the innocent occupants of other vehicles bore the brunt of the trauma while the drunk driver walked away with barely a scratch. "I get that you two were best friends and you might've been close to finding something on Einhorn, but her death doesn't sound like a homicide."

"There's something you don't know. Dani was an alcoholic," she said as though the statement refuted the facts.

"More proof that substantiates what I'm saying."

"You don't understand. She's been sober for seven years. No relapses. Worked the program consistently. Went to meetings once a week like clockwork. There's no way Dani was drinking and driving."

"Alcoholics relapse all the time. Addiction can be a daily struggle for some."

Summer sighed, shoulders slumping, brow creasing, mouth twisting into an expression that tugged at something inside his chest. "I'm used to the skepticism from everyone in town, but I didn't think I'd get it from her family who was sent here to help."

"Yes, I'm family. I'm also a cop." A good one, too. He'd worked for the DCI, a division of the Wyoming State Attorney General's Office, for ten years. At thirty-one, he'd dedicated a third of his life to law enforcement. It was a part of who he was. "I need to look at this objectively. Filter out emotion. The fact is Dani had the added pressure of losing her father and the strain of the farm not making money. Stressful reasons that could drive someone to fall off the wagon. I can't ignore it."

Summer put a hand on his forearm. "I loved Dani like a sister. I knew her. We told each other everything. No matter how embarrassing or shameful. You have to believe me. She wasn't drinking."

No one could say with certainty what a person did alone at home behind closed doors, no matter how well they knew the other person. Countless times he'd seen family members and friends of victims and criminals who were shocked to learn the truth about people they loved.

But he hadn't come all this way to simply shut Summer down. "Let's say you're right and there was foul play. Why would Einhorn Industries kill her?"

"Einhorn has a foothold in the northwestern region. They recently signed a huge government contract. Losing a class action lawsuit would expose them to billions of dollars in damages that they don't want to pay and give the government grounds to terminate that lucrative contract. They're not a behemoth like some other companies who can afford to take that kind of hit or hire lobbyists to champion their side in Washington, DC. This would bankrupt Einhorn."

"That's definitely a motive. I'm sure the list of suspects won't be a short one." It would most likely include the entire executive leadership: CEO, CFO, CCO, CIO, etc. "Not that any of the suits would get their hands dirty. They would delegate the unpleasantness to someone on the security team or a freelance person. All hard to prove *if* a homicide had been committed." A big if with a capital *I*.

Summer tightened her grasp on his arm. "I realize you're inclined to believe Dani's death was an accident. The story is a good one. A recovered alcoholic has a relapse, drinks an abnormally high amount, gets behind the wheel and plows into a tree. Simple. Easy. Won't raise any red flags. Unless you knew Dani. If you did, you'd see it as a *great* cover story for murder. She didn't deserve to die so young."

"No one does."

"I was almost killed tonight because I won't stop asking unwelcome questions about Dani and Einhorn. You saw the guy for yourself."

Someone had tried to kill her and may have very well succeeded if Logan hadn't arrived when he had. That was irrefutable.

He wanted to know who'd attacked her and why. Motives weren't always obvious. Part of him considered telling her to go home and let him handle it, but Summer didn't strike him as the sort to be easily dissuaded.

"I did see him and there's no denying he wanted to do you bodily harm. Assuming the gunman's intent was to silence you, he'll try again."

Danger could even follow her back to Seattle. Logan couldn't let that happen. Whoever it was had messed with the wrong woman and the wrong cowboy.

"You're skeptical," she said, "and I understand why, but you came here anyway. All I'm asking is that you help me get to the truth. No matter where it leads."

Her hopeful expression tugged on him. He couldn't remember when he'd last felt needed. *Crucial.* As one of six boys—including his cousin—he was a middle child and had often gotten lost in the shuffle. Never could find his place and had to carve one out for himself. He filled in the gaps. Served where he could when he could.

But this came down to him. Either he helped Summer see this through and kept her alive in the process, or no one else would. "I'll stay and I won't stop digging until we find the truth. Together. I give you my word."

Chapter Four

On a scale of one to ten, this was…unquantifiable. How could she rate this kind of nightmare?

Her best friend had been murdered, she'd been attacked, and a skeptical, distractingly handsome cowboy had agreed to help.

Ouch. She winced when the ER doctor brought the needle near her arm again.

Then she had stitches to add to the list of the things that lowered the scale on the wrong side.

"I haven't even touched you yet," Dr. Payne said.

An apropos name.

Summer stared at the doctor, wishing he'd show her some sympathy. "The thought of the needle going in hurts."

"The anticipation of pain can trigger cortical systems involved in the experience of pain." Dr. Payne drew in a deep breath, his patience beginning to wear thin on his face. "Try looking away."

Summer turned her head and glanced up at Logan.

He gave her a sincere smile. "I could hold your hand if you think it'll help."

"Let's give it a try. Can't hurt. Pun intended."

His smile deepened, along with his dimples, warming something inside her chest as he took her hand.

She squeezed her fingers tightly around his. Staring

at his handsome face while touching him should've been enough of a diversion, but it wasn't. She pictured the needle drawing closer, the sharp tip pricking her skin, and flinched.

Dr. Payne sighed. "I still didn't touch you."

"It's going to be okay," Logan said, patting her leg. His boyish grin was charming enough to sell ice in Antarctica.

She did her best to fix a matching smile on her face, but only managed to give a grimace.

"Since the wound isn't very deep, can you use liquid stitches instead?" Logan asked the doctor.

"I can," Dr. Payne said with a curt nod. "But they're triple the cost. Most folks either can't afford it or don't want the unnecessary expense. So, I don't usually mention it."

Summer didn't realize those were even an option. Anything was better than a needle. Except for a skin stapler. She shivered at the prospect.

"I'll take the liquid stitches," she said. To heck with the cost.

She saved and invested forty percent of her money, a lesson her mom and dad had drilled into her. Another twenty percent, she sent to her parents, to repay them for their contribution to her law school fees, so they could enjoy retirement. Although she denied herself luxury purchases such as designer handbags, a fancy car and thousand-dollar suits, this was one splurge that was worth the expense.

"Okay." The doctor pulled off his latex gloves in a bit of a huff and tossed them in the trash. "Give me a minute and I'll go grab the surgical glue." He pulled back the curtain in the emergency room bay, but he caught a nurse passing by and asked her to get it for him. Folding his arms, he turned back to them. "So, you're the hotshot lawyer from Seattle out here stirring up trouble."

Here we go.

No matter where she went in Cutthroat Creek she received the same unwelcoming spirit. Originally from a small town in Texas that was just outside of San Antonio—a diverse area in the US—she had wondered if the cold shoulder in Montana was because she was a Black woman on her own. Yet, she'd never had a problem when she'd been with Dani. After being here for a couple of weeks, she realized her ethnicity and gender didn't matter. Whenever she ventured out of Cutthroat to a nearby town, like Bitterroot Falls, she was greeted with a smile and treated hospitably. The moment she mentioned Einhorn, however, everything changed, like a glacier magically materialized, frosting over the conversation.

She had hoped there wouldn't be any need to worry about a confrontation at the hospital.

Apparently not. She was right not to let the doctor anywhere near her with a needle.

Summer straightened. "I'm not here to cause any trouble. Only to get to the truth, which shouldn't be a problem for anyone, unless they have something to hide."

"I'm friends with the coroner. He's a good man. Not corrupt like you've insinuated."

"Even good men can falter," she said, "and succumb to pressure." No one was perfect. She'd seen firsthand in other cases just how far and deep the poisonous influence of a big corporation could taint a community.

"Dani Granger's tox screen wasn't tampered with," Dr. Payne said. "The woman was drunk. If crashing into a tree didn't kill, alcohol poisoning surely would've. Fortunately, she only killed herself in the process. Even though the truth is simple and plain to see, I hear you're hell-bent on twisting it to suit your own manipulative purpose."

Gossip spread faster than Ebola in this small town.

Stiffening, she prepared to set him straight about her motive and her theory.

"Dr. Payne," Logan said before she could get a word out, "it's an ethical and legal violation for the coroner to discuss a case with his pals."

The nurse returned and hesitated near the curtain, picking up on the tension in the medical bay.

"The facts were printed in the *Bitterroot Beacon*," the doctor said, referring to the one paper that serviced the entire area of Bitterroot Lake, including Cutthroat, "and he only discussed it with me after the case was *closed*. Officially, I might add, by the sheriff. As I said, he's an upstanding man."

The nurse cleared her throat. "Excuse me, Doc, I have the surgical glue you requested. If you'd like, I can apply it and free you up to handle other things."

"Thank you, I need to call the sheriff and see what's taking him so long to get here to look into this gunshot wound. He should've been here by now." Dr. Payne threw a scowl Summer's way and left.

"Hi," the nurse said, coming in, "sorry about that." Her name tag read Kimimela. She was Native American, at least part Native American, with light brown skin and long hair that flowed down her back in a glossy black sheet. The nurse set the glue on a stainless steel tray and grabbed a set of latex gloves. "I got the impression it might be better if I stepped in."

Her intervention was appreciated. "Thank you. I'm glad I passed on the regular stitches."

Kimimela tugged on the gloves and inspected the wound

the doctor had already cleaned. "Don't worry about Doc." She removed the top to the glue. "He would've given you nice clean stitches even if you did imply that his golfing and hunting buddy was corrupt."

"You'd think I took out a full-page ad in the *Beacon* declaring as much. I only mentioned the idea to one person."

"And who was that?" Logan asked, still holding her hand like it was the most natural thing in the world.

"The sheriff." Assuming he was on the side of justice, Summer had told him far too much.

"This will sting." Kimimela held up the pen-shaped tube of Dermabond glue. "But it won't last long. I'll line up the edges of the wound and seal it. Should take less than sixty seconds, but the glue needs two to three minutes to dry."

"Should I look away?"

"I overheard how squeamish you were with Doc." The nurse gave a sympathetic look. "While I fix you up, why don't you look at his baby blues?" She gestured to Logan.

Summer met his gaze. He flashed her another easy smile, standing beside her, at ease and composed, with a dark brown cowboy hat on his head and wearing a fresh change of clothes he'd pulled from a duffel bag that looked like it had seen better days.

Since she'd gotten to Cutthroat Creek after Dani's death, her stomach had constantly churned with anxiety and fear while her head filled with ideas of who the murderer could be. With Logan now by her side, for the first time she experienced a sense of calm, a stillness inside. It was as if some great emotional roller coaster, up and down and twisting and turning, had finally stopped.

"Only takes one person," Logan said, "to act as the town crier and then everybody knows your business. It's the same way back home. Small towns have that in common."

A burning sensation flared in her arm, and she grimaced.

He tightened his fingers around hers. "You're almost done and handling it like a champ after the night you've had."

Emotion knotted her throat at his kind words. She drew a quick breath, trying not to notice his sexy lips, the strong jaw, the thick curly hair that fell over his forehead.

Maybe she needed to think of Logan as a bodyguard, keep a good solid emotional wall between them. "I'm more like the biggest wimp, but I appreciate the encouragement."

"Finished. We just need to let it dry," Kimimela said, stepping around to the other side of the stainless steel table.

Logan moved in front of her, leaned over and blew on her shoulder the way her mom used to whenever she got a boo-boo. It helped. A lot.

He really was sweet. Sexy, too.

And cracks already started forming in that wall.

"I read about your lawsuit," Kimimela said. "Is it true about Einhorn products not being safe?"

"It's true. Dani's family stopped using their products, but runoff from their facility contaminated the creek her cattle drank from. The cattle started dying. Tumors. Black teeth. Some of them acted crazed. The ones that lived had to be put down and her father died from cancer."

Summer was tightening the threads that connected directly to Einhorn. Not a simple, quick or straightforward task. After filing the lawsuit, Einhorn had complied with the discovery process and sent her boxes upon boxes of documents she still had to finish going through.

"Einhorn's facility isn't far from the Bigfork Reservation," Kimimela said. "The Snowberry Creek that runs through the Granger property and right next to the facility feeds into the Bigfork River. Is it possible people on the reservation could be poisoned?"

Summer nodded. "It's possible."

"You should be careful if you're planning to stay in town." Kimimela unwrapped a bandage and put it on Summer's arm, covering the liquid adhesive stitches. "You're upsetting the wrong people. Powerful people."

"People willing to kill Dani Granger to silence her?" Logan asked.

The nurse rocked back, her face paling. "I'm not saying that. It's just…" Kimimela peeked out of the bay and looked around. "I knew Dani. We weren't close friends or anything, but we spoke in passing, asked each other about our families. I'd see her around all the time." Kimimela hesitated, pressing her lips in a grim line.

Summer had questioned enough witnesses to know when someone was taking the scenic route to get to the destination of what they wanted to share. "It's okay. Whatever you have to say will stay between us."

Kimimela leaned in and lowered her voice. "I don't know about the tox screen or if Dani was drinking that night, but it was odd she was driving that old Ford pickup."

"The green one?" Logan asked, and Kimimela nodded. "Why would it be odd?"

"That truck was her dad's. Dani never drove it. Not once in the past twelve years since we all got our licenses, around the same time, have I ever seen her behind the wheel of it."

A chill washed over Summer. During the times when she had visited, Dani hadn't used the green truck. In fact, she hated it and had told Summer it represented everything that was wrong with Cutthroat Creek. *Old body style and engineering that was a nose-thumb to social consciousness.*

Logan let go of her hand and stepped closer to the nurse. "Why would the coroner lie about her death?"

"I'm not saying he lied. For all I know, Dani was blitzed out of her mind and made the regrettable choice to drive when she shouldn't have. All I'm saying is Dani wouldn't have done it in that truck. Listen, no one questions the coroner's assessment. Ever. Greg Genberg has been around a long time. Like the sheriff. And this is an election year. Einhorn is a major campaign donor to parties they—"

"Kimi Anne Wheeler." Sheriff Tofteland entered the bay, his voice stern and booming with authority. "Dr. Payne thought you'd be finished by now. He needs your assistance. A young man was just brought in with a broken arm and busted jaw. Brawl in a bar. That's what delayed me in getting here."

The nurse flushed. "I was just, um, explaining the lay of the land."

"No need to do that, Kimi Anne. If you're done in here, you should get going."

The nurse nodded. "Yes, Sheriff." She looked at Summer. "Keep the wound dry for the next few days. The stitches will fall off naturally after it has done its job. Good luck." She hurried off out of the medical bay.

Then Lester Tofteland turned his full, steely focus on Summer. The sheriff had a menacing air of authority to him that made her want to cringe, but she refused to be intimidated, scared off, or browbeaten.

Straightening, she faced him. She wasn't leaving Cutthroat Creek until she decided it was time to go.

THE SHERIFF STARED at Summer and shook his snow-white head with a look of disapproval.

Tofteland, who Logan took to be in his late sixties, cut

the very image of a vintage cowboy with his barrel chest, sweeping walrus-style mustache that was equally white, and pale green eyes lined with wrinkles from all the years of squinting beneath the rim of his campaign hat.

A shadow of anxiety passed over Summer's face as she stiffened, and Logan found himself taking a defensive posture at her side before he even realized what he was doing. He was glad he'd changed his clothes prior to coming to the hospital so he didn't have to face the sheriff looking like a drowned cat.

"Miss Stratton, it appears that you just can't stay out of trouble. This is a sure sign that it's time for you to pack your bags, get out of my town, and go home, missy." The condescending tone grated on Logan.

Two things he couldn't stand: inappropriate assumptions and bullies. Especially bullies wearing a badge.

"Thank you for responding to the gunshot wound as quickly as possible," Logan said, drawing the sheriff's gaze. "*Ms.* Stratton was attacked and nearly killed." *Miss* sounded just as patronizing as *missy*, coming from the sheriff. "I sustained injuries myself during an altercation with the gunman. We'd like to file a report."

Tofteland raised a bushy white eyebrow. "And you are?"

"Logan Powell." Rather than shake hands, he unclipped his badge from his waistband and held it up. "A special agent with DCI."

The sheriff's gaze lasered in on the seven-pointed star. Then he studied Logan for a moment and narrowed his green eyes. "You're outside of your jurisdiction, son."

"That may be, but I'm not your son and she's not a missy. We'd like to file a report about the attack."

"An attack, huh?" The sheriff stroked his mustache.

"Where did this alleged attack take place?" he asked, pulling out a notepad and pen.

Summer folded her hands in her lap. "I was inside the Granger house when—"

"Hold on." The sheriff raised his palm. "Let me stop you right there because we seem to have a failure to communicate. The last time you were out there, I told you that you were trespassing and to steer clear of the Granger property. Otherwise, I'd arrest you."

"Ric Granger called your office," she said, "and left a message that I had permission to be in the house."

The sheriff shrugged. "I never got the message and I can't just take your word for it, little lady."

Logan clenched his jaw, letting the man dig a deeper hole.

"That's why I also advised Mr. Granger to email you. He cc'd me. I'd be happy to pull it up for you."

"I would need to see signed documentation." Tofteland put a fist on his hip. "Emails can be hacked."

What on earth was he implying? Whatever the illicit insinuation, it was ticking Logan off. "Fortunate for you, Sheriff, I'm here."

"And how is your presence fortunate, Mr. Powell?"

"I forgot to mention I'm Dani Granger's cousin. In the glove compartment of my truck, parked just outside, is permission for both me and Ms. Stratton to have full access to the property," Logan said. "Signed by my uncle, the current owner, notarized and witnessed by the mayor back home." He left out the part about the mayor being his mother.

"Also done under my advisement." The distinct hint of satisfaction in Summer's voice almost made Logan smile.

He had thought the document was overkill, along with the limited power of attorney his uncle had given him, but it was coming in handy now.

"I see." The sheriff stroked his mustache again. "Well, let's hear your statements."

They both explained what happened, giving as many details as possible without mentioning anything after the assailant ran off, when Summer had pepper-sprayed him.

"Neither of you got a look at him or noticed any identifying marks, is that correct?" Sheriff Tofteland asked.

Summer nodded.

"That's correct, but I stabbed him in the right wrist," Logan added. "He'll have a wound."

"Not much else to go on besides the assailant's injury." Tofteland hurriedly flipped the notebook closed. "I do have one more thing to ask you, Miss Stratton. What on earth were you doing in the house, creeping around in the dark, at eleven thirty at night?"

The first good question from the sheriff. Logan looked at Summer, wanting an answer as well.

"I was in the dark because I believed the house was being watched. Or I was being followed. I wasn't sure."

"The reason you were there?" Tofteland pressed.

Summer squared her shoulders. "I missed Dani," she said with a little hike of her chin. "We had a pair of blue jeans we used to share, sending them back and forth to each other over the years. I figured I'd get in, find them and go back to the place I'm renting. It was sentimental and silly, but I needed those jeans." Emotion vibrated through the words that flowed smooth as silk from her, like a prepared oral argument.

Frowning, the sheriff shook his head. "Women," he said under his breath, not nearly low enough.

The sheriff might have bought her story, but Logan didn't. He imagined that was how Summer presented herself in court. Confident and calculated, only showing enough emotion to be persuasive.

Tofteland shoved his notebook and pen in his pocket. "You're ruffling a lot of feathers in this town with your lawsuit and your questions. I'm telling you again, for your own safety, you should go home."

"And if she doesn't?" Logan asked.

"This is big sky country. We don't take kindly to outsiders wreaking havoc. I'm not sure I can guarantee her safety unless she leaves."

To Logan, big sky country meant untamed landscape and Old West values—loyalty, respect, justice—where someone's word was their bond—and the folks were warm and welcoming.

Not lawlessness without consequences.

"We're only asking you to do your job," Summer said.

"Whoever broke into the house and attacked you was probably just trying to scare you," the sheriff said. "Next time, their intent could be more deadly."

Logan shook his head. "The intent was clearly deadly tonight." Summer was right. The sheriff wasn't going to help. "Who in town would want to hurt her, other than someone on Einhorn Industries' payroll?"

Sheriff Tofteland laughed. The sound was deep and scathing and devoid of humor. "Boy, you're way out of your depth. Most of the town is on Einhorn Industries payroll. The others who aren't reap the benefits of the company being here in some form or fashion."

Logan met the man's hard stare and held it. "Does that include you?"

"Watch yourself," the sheriff said, pointing a finger in his face. "Do me and yourselves a favor. Leave. Special Agent Powell, go home, where you've got jurisdiction. And as for you, little lady, fight your lawsuit in Seattle. No need to wage war in my town."

"I have every reason to stay," Summer said, not backing down, "and no intention of leaving until I get to the bottom of what really happened to Dani." The glimpse of vulnerability she'd shown minutes earlier was gone, replaced by fiery determination. "Why didn't the coroner perform an autopsy?"

"An autopsy is only carried out when a death is suspicious." The sheriff's ferocious scowl deepened. "What happened to Dani Granger is unfortunate. Poor woman just drank too much. Died in a car crash. She had a blood alcohol level that could strip paint. Case closed." Tofteland crossed his arms over his chest as if to punctuate that statement. "You ought to be careful poking your nose where it doesn't belong in Cutthroat Creek. Never know who'll poke back. You two drive safely." He tipped his campaign hat at them and left.

Logan turned to Summer. "Was he serious that it could've been anyone from town who attacked you?"

"Not only who attacked me, but also killed Dani. The list of possible suspects is longer than you might think," Summer said. "After being here for a couple of weeks, I don't know if it was Einhorn for certain or simply someone in town who was angry at Dani for pursuing a lawsuit."

This conspiracy theory was growing, getting more concrete and feeling less like a far-fetched plot. "Why would a lawsuit against Einhorn make someone in town angry enough to kill Dani and attack you?"

"Dani and I spearheaded this. Einhorn practically owns Cutthroat Creek and dozens of other small towns just like it. Here, the paper mill and the waste recycling plant do in fact provide seventy-five percent of the town's jobs. If

Einhorn lost a lawsuit that's worth billions, bankrupting them, it means a lot of people here would lose their jobs and wouldn't be able to feed their families. I've learned there are plenty of folks in town who will do anything to prevent that from happening. Who hold us responsible."

"Another valid motive, but—"

"No more buts."

"I believe you that there's more here than meets the eye. *But* we need evidence."

Summer got down off the hospital bed. "We're not going to find it here tonight. It's after one in the morning. We need to get some sleep."

"Agreed. Your car is still in the woods near the house. Why don't you just stay there with me tonight. Take one of the guest rooms or Dani's. That way I know you're safe. In the morning, I can follow you over to the cabin you rented."

Summer hesitated like she was going to fight the issue, but to his surprise she said, "Okay." She grabbed her purse. "Let's go."

"Hey," he said, putting a light hand on her uninjured shoulder. For some reason, he just couldn't stop touching her. "What was with that story about the pair of jeans?"

"What makes you think it was a story?"

He gave her an incredulous look. "Come on."

"It was from a movie that Dani and I watched together one night in college. *The Sisterhood of the Traveling Pants.* Ever seen it?"

"Sounds like a sappy flick for teenage girls."

"Don't knock it until you've tried it." She smiled, and he barely resisted the urge to push back stray curls veiling one eye.

They were practically strangers, but the sensation that he'd known her forever crashed through him. Like they'd been something more in a past life. Not that he put a drop of credence in any of that woo-woo pishposh.

She was beautiful. Had the kind of face he could look at forever. And nice. Brave, too, the way she'd attacked him, trying to defend herself.

Still, it was more than a primal attraction. He just couldn't quite put his finger on what *it* was. Maybe all the adrenaline flooding his system induced this visceral reaction, making him feel something that wasn't real.

Only one way to find out. Digging into the circumstances of Dani's death alongside her meant he'd get a chance to know her better.

"The movie has a little something for everyone," she said. "At the heart of it, it's about learning to appreciate what's right in front of you as well as new experiences."

He didn't need a movie for that. Only more time with Summer. "So, what were you really doing in the house, close to midnight and in the dark?"

"The part about being followed or the house being watched was true. Before Dani was killed, she believed someone was following her, too. Her house was even broken into. Everything she had on the case was either in the dining room or stored in the garage. Someone took files, destroyed samples she had collected on her cows, and stole her laptop. Anyway, she started hiding things. *In the house.* I was looking for evidence. Dani told me that she got the last thing we needed. In essence, the smoking gun with Einhorn's prints all over it. We just need to find it."

Something told Logan that would be easier said than done.

Chapter Five

Spending the night at the Granger house had been a good suggestion by Logan. Summer had been reluctant to stay there after Dani's death, but it had been tolerable in the guest room. She still hadn't slept soundly, tossing and turning throughout the night. Although, with Logan close by, just in the next room, she'd had one less thing to worry about.

All her personal things were back at the rented cabin. She'd had to borrow one of Dani's nightgowns to sleep in. A long, white one dappled with yarrow and coneflowers, and with spaghetti straps and ruffles at the bottom. The night-gown had been one of her best friend's favorites. Unlike the fake story about a pair of blue jeans they'd shared, wearing the nightgown had somehow made her feel closer to Dani.

Summer finished changing into her clothes from the day before. Aching to shower and put on a fresh outfit, she tied her hiking boots.

Having slept with her hair up to maintain her curls, Summer pulled out the pins and tossed them back in her purse. As she left the bedroom, Logan was coming up the stairs and had reached the top landing.

Face flush and chest bare, he wore running shorts and sneakers. His tanned skin glistened with sweat.

Summer quickly popped a piece of peppermint gum in

her mouth. "I didn't hear you leave the house," she said, doing her best not to ogle him.

"Went for a quick jog around the property. After my eleven-hour drive up here from Laramie last night, I needed it. I didn't want to wake you, but I left a note for you downstairs so you wouldn't worry," he said, once again reminding her how considerate he was.

Little things like that mattered. She'd had a date stand her up one time, leaving her sitting in a restaurant waiting for almost an hour because he got caught up at work and forgot about her.

A respectful, thoughtful man such as Logan would've called.

"How did you sleep?" he asked.

"Pretty good." She looked past him at the hole in the wall. Last night that bullet had nearly killed her. "Considering." She gestured to it, one of many.

"The sheriff didn't even bother to come out, take a look, collect any evidence. There are bullets and cartridge casings, ballistic fingerprints all over the place."

She'd warned him. "We can't expect much from Sheriff Tofteland."

"Unfortunately, you're right. That's why I called my boss first thing this morning and explained the delicate situation. Asked him to reach out to DCI here in Montana to see if they'd be willing to investigate the attack since they're neutral and a special agent was involved. Once he's done talking to someone in investigations, he'll let me know if they're willing to step on some toes out here."

"Very clever." A lot to admire about Logan Powell. When he stood up to Sheriff Tofteland in the emergency room there'd been a steel gleam in Logan's eyes, an unshakable confidence in his tone, a core of strength that she found very, very appealing.

Right along with the rest of him. Her gaze wandered over the sweat-slicked landscape of his body, and she moistened her lips. He was in incredible shape. Muscular arms. Broad shoulders. Tapered waist. Well-defined legs. She'd never seen calves so sculpted.

Being near him stirred sensations and curiosity she did not need stirred. Not at a time like this, when she needed her sole focus to be on investigating. But his good looks and his kindness and strength and the fact that he'd saved her from the masked gunman had her thoughts careening in a sexually charged direction.

At twenty-eight, she was still a virgin and proud to wait for a meaningful experience rather than give in to a carnal moment she might regret. For her, she didn't see anything wrong with waiting rather than rushing, even though her sisters thought she was being ridiculous.

But this was the first time she'd entertained the idea, for a moment anyway, of sleeping with a man she wasn't in a relationship with.

"I'll take a quick shower," he said, "then drive you to your car and make sure you get back to your rental safely. There's fresh coffee downstairs. I made a pot before my run. Should still be hot."

"Thanks." She skirted past him on the landing, catching the scent of him—sweat and musk and all male—and headed down the stairs.

"Don't clean up while you're waiting," he said, and she glanced back at him over her shoulder. "Just in case the Montana DCI decide to come out. It's best to leave the scene as intact as possible."

"Smart thinking. I probably would've tidied up. I hate a mess."

"I'm a clean freak, too." A lopsided grin tugged at one corner of his mouth, highlighting a single dimple.

She had to grab the railing to steady herself on the stairs. "One thing we have in common."

"I'm sure there are many others. Like I remember you told me you were close to your family. Especially your sisters. All of you named after seasons."

How did he recall that after five years?

Summer did miss being near her family in Texas, having weekly dinners with them. Her parents were about to retire and planned to spend the next three years living on a cruise ship, sailing around the world. Winter, a detective with the San Antonio PD, was going to relocate to Seattle to be closer. Her other sister, Autumn, who was a forensic psychologist, was ready to leave the congestion and high prices of Los Angeles, where she currently worked. But Autumn complained Seattle was too rainy and too large and would prefer someplace with small-town values: community involvement, neighborliness, quality family time, resilience and inclusivity. The type of cornerstones they had growing up.

"I'm tight with my family, too," Logan said.

Except for his uncle, but that was a conversation for another time. "All boys, right?"

"Yeah, but almost everybody is engaged or married, so there are plenty of daughters-in-law."

"Does that also include you? I mean, are you engaged? Married?" she asked, noting he didn't have on a wedding band. Not that the lack of one meant he wasn't married. "Attached?"

"Comfortably single."

Nice to know. "Oh. Me, too."

His grin spread into a deep smile.

Why did she say that? Just because she wasn't dating didn't mean she was available for a long-distance relationship and just because he was a nice guy didn't mean he was interested anyway. He did say that he was comfortable being single.

Nothing wrong with getting to know him and being friends with someone she also happened to be attracted to.

"I'll hurry," he said. "I won't be long." He disappeared into the bathroom and the shower started.

It was a good thing she was staying in a cabin on the outskirts of town. She was already going to be attached at the hip to him while they dug deeper into the circumstances surrounding Dani's death. Spending countless hot, sultry nights under the same roof as him, too, would only spell trouble.

The living room was an even bigger disaster in the morning light than she had first imagined. Impossible to get to the kitchen without stepping on something.

She grabbed a mug and poured a cup of hot coffee.

Remnants of pepper spray lingered in the room. To let in much-needed fresh air, she cracked open the window over the sink, which she realized she'd left unlocked after attempting to make her great escape.

Sipping on her coffee, she stared at the fridge, still at an angle, resting between the counters and blocking the back door.

The gunman who broke in had gone through a lot of trouble to push it over that way. Not to mention the noise he had made in the kitchen and the living room. Had he done all that to spook her and draw her out into the open?

"Ready?" Logan asked, appearing in the doorway. He

was fully dressed, in a white T-shirt and jeans, his curly hair damp from his shower.

"Sure." She finished the coffee in her mug, set it in the sink, then closed and locked the window. "We can go."

He let her walk out of the kitchen ahead of him. Passing him on the threshold, she couldn't help taking in the clean, woodsy smell of him that taunted her senses with promises of safety. He trailed behind her through the living room.

Near the front door, she noticed the console table for the entryway. Unopened mail was on top beside a small porcelain bowl with owls painted on it. Inside were Dani's keys.

She picked them up, ran her fingers across them and clenched them in her hand.

"What is it?" Logan asked.

Ideas spun in her head, but she said, "Nothing." She put the keys in her purse.

Outside, they climbed down the porch steps. As they headed toward Logan's big silver Dodge Ram, she stared at Dani's pickup. Black and beat up, it was a Chevy like the old, green two-seater Dani had supposedly been driving the night of her accident, but large enough to haul several passengers along with plenty of farm supplies. Still, it was certainly smaller than the massive Ram they climbed into.

Although it was only nine thirty in the morning, the truck was already steaming hot. Logan rolled down all four windows. The cross breeze was nice as they drove down the driveway and turned onto the road.

Summer took Dani's keys out and stared at the keychain with the name of their alma mater engraved. Shifting in her seat, she angled toward Logan. "I can't stop thinking about what the nurse, Kimi, told us."

"About Dani never driving the green truck?"

"Yeah. It wasn't until she mentioned it that I realized Dani hadn't used that truck during any of my visits. Always steered clear of it. Told me once she hated the old thing."

"I've never known her to use the green truck either, but that doesn't mean that she didn't climb behind the wheel drunk."

"Or maybe someone put her behind the wheel. Someone who grabbed the wrong set of keys from the bowl in the entryway."

"It's also possible Dani took the wrong keys. By the time she stumbled outside, maybe she was too inebriated to care which truck she was driving."

Glancing out the windshield, Summer swallowed a jolt of frustration and shoved Dani's keys back in her purse. "There has to be a way to convince you that Dani didn't have a relapse."

"Actually, there might be," he said, and she looked at him, waiting for him to finish. "If Dani went to meetings regularly, then she had a sponsor. Someone who could verify her consistency and possibly provide firsthand insight about her state of mind in the days leading up to the accident."

Another good idea. "How do you propose we do that? AA is anonymous for a reason."

"This is a small town. Can't be too many meetings. We go to one, around the time it's supposed to end, and talk to the person leading it." Logan slowed, stopping on the road alongside her car.

She had parked her navy sedan off the shoulder in the grass, nestled between two trees.

"You didn't do a very a good job of hiding your vehicle," he said.

In the daylight, it was plain to see. "At night, I figured it wouldn't be so easy to spot since it's a dark color."

"That's true, but when I pulled down the road, your license plate reflected my headlights, and I noticed the car. I didn't put much thought into it at the time since it was late and I was bone-tired from the drive, but anyone looking for you would've seen it. Not only that but with the rain you could've gotten stuck in the mud. Parking there wasn't a good idea all around."

If she had made it to the car last night only to get stuck in the mud, she would've been a sitting duck. A seasoned cop, like her sister Winter, never would've made such a careless mistake. Then again, Winter had warned her not to go to Cutthroat Creek at all. *Better to hire a private investigator.* But a PI would not have been personally invested in the outcome. "I'm a lawyer, not a cop. Staying under the radar isn't really my forte."

"I get it." He flashed another dazzling smile her way. "Stars weren't meant to hide. They were made to shine."

Was he flirting with her? "That's the nicest compliment anyone has ever given me." Even if it was a little cheesy.

"I find that hard to believe. I'm sure you draw compliments like bees to nectar."

Her cheeks heated and she lowered her gaze. "Believe it or not, I don't."

"Guys must tell you that you're beautiful all the time."

He thought she was *beautiful*?

She looked back up at him. "Sometimes. Usually they just say pretty." Not beautiful. "But I've also been called a prude and—my least favorite—a tease." Several men had even been threatened by the fact that not only was she attractive but also an attorney at the top of her game.

"Nothing wrong with being modest and taking things slow. I know a few guys who think that if they buy a woman dinner, they're entitled to more after the meal. In my book, *more* should be hard-earned, like respect."

She tended to keep her virginity a secret from the men she went out with. Never lauded it as a prize for someone to win. But the idea of intimacy being hard-earned, like respect, resonated.

Men who felt entitled were the worst. She had once dated a professional athlete who had demanded sex after their third dinner, insistent to the brink of violence. To this day, she shuddered to think what might have happened if she hadn't been carrying her Mace.

"I dated a guy for four months and we never made it past second base." The words flew out of her mouth without thinking, like a defense mechanism to keep from talking about the close call with the athlete that was now at the forefront of her mind.

"Oh," Logan said, his eyebrows rising like they might jump off his forehead.

"He smelled like oatmeal, and I couldn't get over it." The guy had checked all the boxes on paper. From a good family. Parents still married. Six-figure job with a big tech company. Attractive. Nice. Interested in marriage and kids. She kept hoping things would finally click. But then there'd been that odd scent, and her inability to let her guard down around him, and how he never shared anything deep about himself, like nothing truly deep existed, and the complete lack of any *zing* between them.

Her list of intangible cons exceeded the number of checked boxes.

She didn't buy into the fairy-tale notion of romance. She

understood that perfection in a partner wasn't possible, but she did expect a spark. Passion.

At least butterflies.

And a man needed to smell good.

Even sweaty, Logan smelled tempting enough to contemplate third base.

"Four months is a long time to some people," he said, "but good things come to those who wait."

Thankfully, she had the sense not to mention that she'd never made it beyond second base with *any* guy.

What was it about Logan that had her mind dredging up the past, loosening her lips and pushing her out of her comfort zone?

"Was that your longest relationship?" he asked.

"Yes," she said, and his brows jumped up again, his eyes growing wide. Enough of her dating résumé. If she continued any longer, he'd think she was defective. "So, you'll follow me to the cabin?"

"Yep."

With a nod, she hopped out and hustled through the low brush over to her vehicle. She pulled on the door handle, and it opened without her hitting the key fob.

The door was unlocked. An unnerving feeling swept through her, but maybe she had been in such a rush on her not-quite-so-clandestine mission that she'd forgotten to lock it.

She got in and pushed the start button, turning on the engine. Music flooded the car, contemporary pop from a local station. The same one playing in Logan's truck. He was watching her, tapping his fingers on the steering wheel to the beat. She lowered the volume, cranked the air conditioner and rolled down the windows to let in a breeze on the drive until the AC kicked in, cooling things off.

Summer fastened her seat belt. Putting her hands on the steering wheel, she was about to press on the brake and shift gears when she sensed movement and then felt something brush the cuff of her jeans.

Tensing, she looked down. A snake slithered over her foot—sand-colored with a triangular head and beady, black eyes—hissing as it slunk between her boots.

Her heart seized. A scream lodged in her throat.

Move and you die.

She forced herself to stay still as stone, warring with the fight-or-flight instinct pumping through her system.

"Logan!" she called out, drawing on every ounce of courage she had to remain calm. Slowly, she turned her head, careful not to move any other part of her body, and met his gaze.

"What's wrong?" he asked, peering over at her through his passenger-side window.

"Snake!" Fear fractured the word into three syllables.

Logan jumped out of his truck and was at her door within seconds. He poked his head inside the car, looked down at the footwell and cursed.

"Is it poisonous?" she asked, praying the answer was no.

Please tell me it's a harmless garden snake.

"Venomous, and yes. Highly. Don't move," he said, but he didn't need to tell her that. Logan reached inside the vehicle, hitting the button to unlock all the doors, moving quick as a ghost. Running around to the other side of the car, he yanked open the passenger's side doors, the back followed by the front. Then he moved back around to the driver's side and slowly opened the one behind her. "Listen to me very carefully."

"Okay."

"I'm going to get you out of the car."

Panic threaded through her veins. "No. If I move, it'll bite me."

"You're not even going to lift a finger. I'll take you out, slowly. As long as there are no sudden movements, we'll be fine."

We? She was the one stuck in the car with a deadly snake. "Just call animal control or something."

"That could take an hour. Maybe longer for them to get here," he said, and something inside her chest squeezed, sucking the oxygen from her lungs. "You can't hold still that long."

Stay strong.

Then she glanced back down. The snake's forked tongue stabbed the air, as a spine-tingling hiss curled in her ears. Terror prickled her skin and she nearly flinched.

Blocking it all out, she took in a deep gulp of air, held it a moment and blew out the shaky breath, clearing her head. Logan was right. She couldn't keep that up for an hour, or possibly longer.

"Shoot it," she said, slowly enunciating each word, determined not to let hysteria overrule reason. Damage to her car didn't matter, only staying alive.

"Killing it with a headshot on the first try in tight quarters is not likely." His voice was calm, steady. "I'll only end up aggravating it and provoking the darn thing to bite you. But don't worry. I'm going to do everything possible to make sure nothing happens to you."

"Logan." His name left her lips in a desperate whisper.

"Do you trust me?"

For some reason, the answer was clear and bright as the sun on a cloudless day. "Yes."

"Close your eyes. When I tell you, I want you to go limp and let me do all the work. All right?"

What choice did she have? "Okay."

Fear wormed down her spine. Her heart jackhammering against her sternum, she put her faith in a man she barely knew and shut her eyes.

Chapter Six

A prairie rattlesnake.

Looked to be about five to six feet long. Even though the rattler was deadly, the nature of all snakes was the same. They were defensive rather than offensive creatures. Leave them alone and they sought to avoid confrontations with larger animals such as coyotes, wolves, bobcats and humans.

He'd opened the car doors to give it an escape route. The vast majority of snakebites occurred when people attempted to kill or otherwise catch one.

Then again, he doubted there were any statistics on individuals trapped inside a car with a snake.

Logan grasped the handle of the driver's door and gently lifted it until he heard the soft *click* of the mechanism disengaging. Then slowly, centimeter by centimeter, he opened the door wide. Fortunately, he had almost a full ninety-degree opening to work with.

Crouching low, he watched the rattler slither between her feet, the scaly body trailing over her toes. Its forked tongue darted out as the snake slid under the seat, heading toward the back.

Summer was wearing thick hiking boots. The ridge of the top stopped above her ankles from what he could tell beneath her jeans. A small layer of protection that might make all the difference once he moved her.

"Do nothing," he reminded her. "Let me handle it."

"Got it." Her voice was soft and low.

He inched closer to the frame of the vehicle. Slipping the fingers of his left hand under her thighs, he wiggled them deftly deeper along the seat, one inch at a time, not making a sound, and got a firm grip on the outer edge of her leg. All the while he listened for the warning sound of the snake's rattle, which would tell him if the creature felt surprised or threatened.

So far, only the blissful beat of the music.

Sweat beaded his forehead and rolled down along his temples. Summer held so still she seemed to be holding her breath.

With his other hand, he carefully pried her fingers from the steering wheel, lifting her left arm, and draped it around his neck. He nestled his shoulder up against her side while tracking the snake. The tail had disappeared. Even though the rattler was out of sight, he was 100 percent certain that it was directly under her seat.

He repeated the same process he used to get a hold of her legs, sliding his right hand between her back and the seat and finally under her arm. Once he had a firm grip on her side, right at her rib cage, he said, "Now."

Rigid tension left her body as she sagged against him, her other hand merely cupping the steering wheel now rather than holding it in a death grip.

Gradually, he lifted her from the driver's seat, moving inches in what felt like strained minutes. The distinctive rattle rose from underneath her seat, warning him to stop. It sounded like the buzzing of a large hornet. If the snake had been coiled, giving it height and increasing its striking distance, with the rattled tail completely off the ground, the sound would've been more like that of a pepper grinder.

The rattler was limited in its current position. Better to keep going rather than leave her in the car.

Standing from the crouched position, holding her and shifting her out of the seat—doing so painfully slowly—taxed every fiber of the muscles in his legs and back. Summer was soft, slender and svelte, with the lithe physique of a dancer. He was grateful she was as light as she looked and that he spent so much time getting in hard workouts on his family's ranch.

His muscles quivered. Perspiration dripped down his back. He almost had her free when the rattler struck.

The snake's fangs nipped the sole of her boot as he rushed backward. He got her clear of the car frame and out of striking range, shuffling her a safe distance as quickly as possible on the off chance the snake left the vehicle.

At the front of his truck, he stopped. Holding on to her, he set her feet down on the ground. She opened her eyes and went limp in his arms, her knees buckling. He picked her back up, carried her around to his open driver's-side door and sat her down on the seat.

He cupped her face in his hands. "Breathe. You're going to be all right."

She nodded, but fear still glistened in her eyes.

His heart was racing. He'd never been so terrified of making a mistake in his life as he'd been in the last few minutes. "I'm going to call someone to get the snake out of your car. Okay?"

Another silent nod from her.

But he couldn't let her go yet. He pushed her hair from her face, longing to give her a hug or a kiss, any physical comfort to ease her lingering stress and make things better.

His reaction to her was unsettling. While working he never had trouble disconnecting when dealing with a victim or handling a case. But this was different.

Summer threw off his entire center of gravity.

Get a grip and focus.

Finally, he forced himself to pull away. He hurried back to her vehicle and slammed the doors, keeping the rattler contained inside. Once someone came to the scene, he wanted an official report of the snake being in her car.

He whipped out his phone and placed a call to animal control.

By the time he was back beside her, his shirt was damp with perspiration.

She climbed over into the passenger's seat, making room for him. He hopped inside, closed the door and rolled up the windows.

The air conditioner blasted cold air from the vents, cooling them both off. Not only from the July heat but also from the boiling tension of the too-close encounter with the rattler.

"Are you okay?" he asked. The silence from her was concerning.

"Yeah. Fine."

But she didn't look fine at all. "Someone will be here soon to take care of the snake. There's an agent already in the area. Something to do with a bear."

"Thank you for coming to my rescue. Again. Twice in two days."

Less than twelve hours apart, to be more precise. "Starting to become a habit."

She grimaced. "Let's hope not. As much as I appreciate you being there for me, I'd prefer not to be in a position where I need to be saved."

Thinking about it, he had to agree. "I can't believe how still and calm you were through that."

"Calm?" she scoffed. "What you witnessed was barely contained hysteria."

"Could've fooled me. Faced with a scary, life-threatening situation like that, people often panic and do something stupid." Her levelheaded reaction was a testament to how well she was able to perform under pressure.

"Thank you, I guess."

It was definitely another compliment. "You did good," he said. "Seriously."

Summer was tough. On the outside, she appeared ladylike, almost delicate, but she had a backbone of steel.

"No, you're the one who did great," she insisted. "Getting me from the car without a single bite."

"Well, you did get one. On your boot. Good thing you were wearing those thick-soled hiking shoes, and that rattler couldn't coil under the seat and strike up."

Luck had been on their side. If the snake had still been in the footwell, Logan wouldn't have been able to get her free from the car safely.

"Once you got me out, why didn't you just kill it rather than calling animal control?" she asked.

"Two reasons. First, I want it officially documented by someone other than the sheriff's department that the snake was in your car. And second, it didn't mean any harm. Snakes are good for the environment. They help prevent diseases from spreading and play an integral role in maintaining a healthy ecosystem."

"Of course, a cowboy from Wyoming would know all about them. Fortunate for me. I don't know what I would've done if I had been alone."

The notion of losing her was enough to make his stomach churn. He reached across the console and took her hand. She threaded her fingers with his. The connection between them was already growing and he wanted to see what it could blossom into.

"What's the survival rate for a snakebite?" she asked.

"Depends on how many times you're bitten and how quickly antivenom is administered. Even if you survive, you're looking at days, possibly a week in the hospital."

"The entire time you were trying to get me out of the car safely, I kept wondering how that snake got in my vehicle in the first place," she said. "What are the odds of that happening by chance? Some weird fluke? Is that normal for a snake to be able to get into your car?"

"There are nine or ten snake species in Montana." More in Wyoming, eighteen that he knew of. "But the only venomous one is that prairie rattlesnake that was in your car. I'd say that'd put the odds at zero of it being a fluke." Making documentation of the incident all the more important.

Squeezing her eyes closed for a moment, Summer pressed her lips in a firm line. "Do you think the guy who attacked me at the house put it in there?" she asked, looking back at him.

"Working a case is often like piecing together a jigsaw puzzle. While I was out on my run this morning, I thought about the disarray in the house and the way you were attacked. Pieces that make more sense now. To answer your question, yes, I believe whoever attacked you planted the snake in your car. I think he never intended to graze you with the bullet. His goal was to get you moving. He blocked the back door in the kitchen to force you to flee from the front and head straight for your vehicle. When you came down the steps, why didn't you run out of the house?"

She dropped the back of her head against the seat. "I

left my purse and car keys in the living room. I had to go in there to get them."

"A hiccup the guy probably hadn't counted on. Much like me showing up." Thank goodness he arrived when he did. That he hadn't made an extra pit stop to refuel and stretch his legs and instead had pushed on through to get to the house. Ten minutes later and the outcome might have been far different. "He probably figured you'd be scared half to death, racing for your car, that you'd hop in and speed off in the dark, not aware that you had a deadly passenger on board until it was too late. Either the snake would've killed you or a frenzied car crash."

Logan needed to update his boss. He let go of Summer's hand and started typing him a text message. In case DCI here in Montana needed a bigger push to investigate, this latest incident should be enough to get them involved.

"There's one thing I can't wrap my head around. Why would that guy go through all the effort when he could've simply shot me, put a bullet in my head and been done with it?" she asked.

"Then the sheriff would've been forced to do his job." No way to turn a blind eye to cold-blooded murder. "If your theory is correct that Dani wasn't drinking and driving and was really killed, then I guess it would be for the same reason. The coroner, Genburg, would've signed off on your death certificate, ruling the cause a snakebite or another fatal crash, and your murder would've looked like an accident. Like Dani's."

She wrapped her arms around herself and rubbed her arms. "This is worse than I thought."

Summer had no idea how ugly this was shaping up to be, and he wasn't sure if he should share his suspicion.

The high level of planning involved, blocking the kitchen

door with the fridge, shooting to scare her rather than kill her, deliberately slipping the venomous snake in her car, and the high likelihood that she had been followed, all pointed to one thing.

He didn't want to jump to conclusions, but his gut told him that a professional, someone accustomed to eliminating targets, had Summer in their crosshairs.

Chapter Seven

The animal control agent had confirmed that—while it was easy, though not likely, for a snake to get into the engine bay, seeking a dark place to hide from predators—it was near impossible for the prairie rattlesnake to get inside the cabin of the vehicle. Unless Summer had left the windows down or doors open in a wooded area for an extended period of time.

None of which she had done.

Summer parked her car in front of the small guest cabin she'd rented through Airbnb for the month. The place was nestled between Cutthroat Creek and the town of Bitterroot Falls, close enough to the former for folks to consider it the outskirts.

It was peaceful out here and one of the most scenic parts of Montana, though there were quite a few to choose from. Far prettier than back home in Texas and drier than Seattle. The cabin was adjacent to the owner's main house and faced a massive, pristine lake with crystal blue water and a backdrop of majestic mountains and cherry orchards. The sight of the water rose up to meet her, the lake only a stone's throw away. Staying here lightened her grief over Dani and helped her reconnect to her cowboy roots. A culture she missed after years trapped in Seattle with horrible traffic, earthquakes, prevalent homelessness and high housing costs.

Once the lawsuit was done and she'd gotten to the bottom of Dani's death, maybe she'd come back on vacation and soak it all in. Take the chance to enjoy herself. She hadn't had a fun break since graduating from law school. It was long overdue, and this was as close to paradise as one could get.

She got out of the car and inhaled. The air was perfumed by bougainvillea and clematis growing around the cabin.

"Amazing view of Bitterroot Lake and the mountains," Logan said, coming up alongside her. "I bet the fishing is great." He turned to her. "Do you fish?"

"A little. More so when I was younger and spent time on my cousin's ranch." The Kings on her mother's side. "They had a huge pond full of fish. I remember it being quite relaxing." Fond memories of being on the ranch. They had their fair share of snakes in Texas, harmless and venomous alike. Not once had she come across one and certainly no deadly encounters. "I believe there's trout and bass in this lake."

"If I lived out here," he said with a bright smile, like he was fantasizing, "I'd go fishing once a week during the season. Food always tastes better when you catch it yourself." He took a deep breath. "This is a little slice of *paradise*."

She'd thought the exact same thing. The sun shimmering on the vast expanse of the water. Flowers and blooming trees near the shore. Mountains not too far in the distance teasing the idea of a long hike. Sunset was primetime perfection. "That's how I feel." Maybe it was time to update her checklist on what she was looking for in a partner. Include a box for someone who saw the world the way she did and wanted a similar lifestyle. "Pictures online didn't do the place justice." She was fortunate to have stumbled on it during her search.

Logan looked around, his attention landing on the main house. "Are the owners around all the time?"

"No. I haven't seen them since I checked in," she said, walking down the driveway to pick up a copy of that morning's *Bitterroot Beacon*. "They delayed their trip to visit family in Florida to give me the keys and show me around a bit. They even took me to lunch at a fantastic lodge down the road within walking distance." Then she'd shared her reasons for her indefinite stay. Their smiles had faded and their demeanors turned icy. "The food is so good I've eaten there every day."

A worried expression crossed his face. "You're out here by yourself?"

Yes and no. "The neighbors are fairly close. Not quite shouting distance, but easy enough to reach." She could at least see their houses. "And the owners here were kind enough to introduce me before they left." Everyone was lovely. At first. Standoffish once they realized who she was and why she was there, but she believed they'd help her if she had to turn to them in a bind.

Logan scrubbed a hand across his jaw like he was thinking. "I need to look into Einhorn's top brass, see if I can find any leads for us."

"Done. I already have a file on them. Started digging after Dani told me she thought she was being followed."

"Good." But he didn't sound relieved as he kept looking around the property. His phone chimed. He took it out and read the text.

"Is that your boss getting back to you?" she asked.

"Uh, no," he said, like the question had pulled him from his thoughts. "On the drive over, I heard back from him."

"And?"

"The Montana DCI has agreed to investigate the attack last night. My boss requested someone not originally from these parts, if possible. They're going to send Special Agent Declan Hart. He's from Colorado and has been with the department five years. The text message is actually from him. Agent Hart plans to be at the house at three o'clock today to collect forensic evidence."

"At least that's a spot of good news." She went to the front door, unlocked it and let him go in ahead of her.

He crossed the threshold, staggered to a halt and stared at the piles of boxes she had stacked everywhere. "What's all this?" he asked.

"In order to help get proof against Einhorn, I filed the lawsuit and this is one result."

"Don't you need proof before you sue a company?"

Once again, the answer was yes and no. "Dani had already been collecting evidence on her end, but it wasn't enough," she explained. "When you file a lawsuit, it triggers the discovery process that forces a company to disclose everything." She waved her hand at the boxes crowding the small cabin. "And they sent me absolutely everything. I've been going through it on my own for months. My firm hasn't been too happy with me. I was on the fast track to becoming the youngest partner until all this." Now she was in danger of losing her job. She'd already taken two pay cuts as this case sucked up all her time. "Since I didn't know how long I was going to be out here investigating Dani's death, I had the records shipped here, so I could continue working on them."

"You barely have any room to walk around. There was no place else you could store them?"

"I filed the suit in conjunction with a local attorney.

The one guy willing to risk attaching his name to it over in Bitterroot Falls. Jeff Arbuckle. He was supposed to help me find somewhere to put everything, but I haven't heard back from him yet. I should check in and see if he's found any possibilities."

"I might know someone who could solve this problem for you," Logan said.

"Really? Who?" she wondered.

"Chance Reyes. He's a lawyer, like you. Works for Ironside Protection Services. IPS has an office in Bitterroot Falls. Chance and I grew up together. His family's ranch is adjacent to mine. In fact, the two have been combined since his sister married my eldest brother, Monty, last year." His brow crinkled, giving her the impression that there was more to the nuptials that didn't make him happy. "I'll give him a call and see if he can help us out."

Us. She liked the idea of not being in this on her own. "You get along with Chance, but not his sister?"

"Amber? No, she's great." Deep creases etched his forehead again, this time accompanied by a tense smile. "We're, um, good friends."

Huh. Maybe there was a problem with the in-laws. Plenty of books and movies dramatized how disastrous those relationships could be. "Are the Reyes parents a nightmare?"

"They're deceased, but when they were alive our families were both quite close."

Odd. She couldn't help feeling like she was missing something.

Logan started taking pictures with his cell phone.

"What are you doing?" she asked.

"When I tell Chance that we need storage room, I want him to know what to expect."

We. She smiled. "Good idea. The only problem is that I

have a system." Only she knew which boxes she'd already sorted through, which ones she considered a higher priority. "I'll need to label them or put sticky notes on them so that they don't get all mixed up."

"I'll text Chance the pictures and give him a call while you freshen up."

"Right." She took the narrow path through the maze of boxes from the living room to the kitchen. "Do you want me to start a pot of coffee before I shower?" she asked. Summer could drink coffee all day long. It was a great appetite suppressant that kept her focused.

"No, thanks," he called out from the front of the cabin. "I figured we could grab a bite to eat once you were ready to go."

Sounded perfect. She was famished. "Want some water?" she asked, peeking around a stack of boxes to see him as she waited for an answer.

He took out his phone and started dialing. "I'm all right for now. No need to worry about me but I appreciate you asking."

Opening the fridge, she took a bottle of water out and sipped it. After the incident with the snake her throat was achy and dry.

"I got his voicemail," Logan said. "I'll leave a message."

Summer slipped off the rubber band from the newspaper while Logan left a brief voicemail that conveyed the urgency of the situation. Flipping through the paper had become a part of her morning routine since she'd been there. She glanced at the front-page headline.

Local Man Drowns in Bitterroot Lake.

She turned to the story and choked on the water sliding down her throat.

"Oh my God." A glacial chill went through her as if

someone had walked over her grave. She couldn't believe what she was reading.

"Are you okay? Something wrong?" Logan asked, putting his phone away.

She hurried over to him, winding her way through the labyrinth of obstacles, and showed him the front page of the *Beacon*. "Jeff Arbuckle, the lawyer I was working with, is dead. He drowned in a boating accident while he was out on the lake two days ago."

Logan took the newspaper from her and glanced over the story. "Says he was alone. Fishing at night."

"How much do you want to bet that it wasn't accident?"

"Some people fish at night. Plenty of species are more active at that time, like bass," Logan said.

Sighing, she bit down on her impatience.

He looked up at her. "But I agree that another supposedly accidental death is too much of a coincidence. I don't think that it's a good idea for you to stay out here alone."

"All the documents are here. We don't know if Chance has space for them. I usually review what I can at night until I'm ready to go to bed. The place is paid for until the end of the month." She might have spent one night at Dani's house, but she wasn't mentally prepared to stay there for however long this was going to take.

Logan put a hand on her arm and rubbed, the gesture a comforting one. "We'll work out the logistics of everything. I promise," he said. "Whoever attacked you last night may be tying up loose ends and I don't think he's done with you. Pack a bag. After everything that's happened, you can't be here alone."

Chapter Eight

Sitting in his truck, parked behind a church, Logan read through the file on Einhorn higher-ups that Summer had compiled. Summer kept track of the time. At one o'clock, a local AA meeting was scheduled to let out. In case it ended early, they planned to head over a few minutes beforehand to the auxiliary building where the group met.

Logan glossed over the information regarding the CEO and founder Evan Einhorn and COO Todd Collins, along with the rest of the usual suspects. No doubt if Einhorn was producing toxic fertilizer, the leadership was aware of it and might have even taken steps to make the problem disappear. Billions were at stake. But the suits weren't the ones doing the dirty work. They needed to find the gunman to connect the attack to Einhorn, or whoever was responsible.

He focused on the last name in the file. Emma Einhorn. CSO—Chief Security Officer. "What is Ms. Einhorn's relationship with the CEO?"

"Emma is his daughter."

Logan nodded. "Then this is more than a job for her. It's personal. With her father as the founder and CEO, the company is her family's legacy. A powerful thing that many people would go to ugly lengths to protect."

"You sound as if you have firsthand knowledge of something like that."

"I watched my own parents push moral boundaries to ensure the Shooting Star Ranch survived for future generations. They conspired with Mr. Reyes to force Monty to marry Amber." That was the simplest explanation.

"I thought the marriage was happy."

"It is. Now. This was ten years ago. Caused a lot of pain. Mostly for Amber. But it all worked out in the end. She and Monty are deeply in love. They have a beautiful son. The two ranches are also joined. The Shooting Star-Longhorn. Everything worked out the way it was supposed to, but sometimes even the best people will cross the worst lines to preserve a legacy."

"Okay, Emma Einhorn has a motive beyond money, her family's legacy, but she may also have the means." Summer took the sheet of paper from him, turned it over and pointed out a paragraph in her bio.

"Emma used to be a detective with the Pondera Pines PD. Okay, so what?"

"The entire security team has four people, including her. Charles Boyd, the deputy CSO, Alex Pope and Tyler Higgins. Guess what they all have in common?"

An answer popped into his head, but that couldn't be right. "They're not all former cops, are they?"

"They are. Guess what else?"

"You've got me waiting in suspense." Shifting in his seat toward her, he leaned closer, truly riveted by the sparkle in her eyes and what she had to say next.

Summer rested her forearm on the console between them, angling to face him, giving him a tempting view of her cleavage in the pale blue V-neck top that clung to her frame like a second glove. Her perfume scented the cool air of the cabin. Sensual sandalwood, freesia and jasmine.

Complex and sophisticated without being overpowering. Suited her perfectly.

"Go on, tell me," he prompted.

"They were all fired. At the same time."

She definitely knew how to pique his interest.

"Any idea why?" he asked.

"I did some digging."

"Of course you did." His gaze dropped to her slender, shapely legs exposed in sexy pleated shorts. Her skin looked smooth as satin. He bit the inside of his cheek, longing to run his hand along her thigh to see how soft and supple it really was. "And you found?"

"An article came out in the *Beacon* six months prior to their dismissal. Two suspects died under suspicious circumstances while in police custody, while in their custody to be more specific. They were subsequently suspended during the investigation. Rumors of corruption filled the paper. The county coroner, ole Genburg, stated the manner of death was an accident. The families filed a civil suit for wrongful death. As a result, PPPD fired the officers for not following police procedure. A settlement was reached with the families for an undisclosed amount. But would you like to know for how much?"

"Didn't you just say it was undisclosed?" he said while daring to put his arm on the console beside hers, skin to skin. She was warm and soft.

"I did." Crossing her legs, she flashed a coy smile. *Beautiful.* "How did you find out?"

"I visited one of the families and simply asked. A widow. Each family received a quarter million dollars."

"Surely they signed NDAs." Such deals were usually made in the shadows on the condition that no one leaked the details.

"I told the woman to give me a dollar, thereby retaining me as her lawyer, which made her free to disclose the amount to me under attorney-client privilege."

"Shrewd. I like it." He liked her. *Very much.*

"A month after the settlement was announced, Evan Einhorn donated a half million to Pondera Pines."

"Convenient."

"I think it's a little too convenient. Then he hired his daughter and her cronies."

"When did all this take place?"

"Four years ago." She glanced down at her watch. "I think it's time we should head inside."

As they climbed out of his truck, his cell phone rang. He pulled it from his pocket. "Hey, Chance," Logan said, walking beside Summer toward the auxiliary building located behind the church. "Thanks for getting back to me."

Never a doubt in Logan's mind that Chance would. Not only were they close friends but their families' histories were also intricately woven together. Chance always appreciated how Logan supported his sister Amber, had her back no matter what. Growing up, Logan had thought he was in love with Amber, would've done anything for her, but she had only had eyes for his older brother Monty. She'd made her choice painfully clear a lifetime ago. Logan had had ten years to lick his wounds from the rejection. It no longer stung. Now Monty and Amber were married and had a baby. He wished his brother and sister-in-law every happiness. They were meant to be. If only he wasn't forced to see it every day on the ranch, where they all lived.

He was ready for a clean slate. One in which he defined his identity, and nobody thought of him as lovelorn Logan. As Monty's little brother. As Amber's spurned admirer. As the one son who didn't have the joy of ranching flowing in his veins. As the family stopgap.

A new place that felt like home, where he could crawl out from under the Powell shadow.

"Sorry I couldn't return your call sooner," Chance said. "We just wrapped up a couple of cases."

"Satisfied clients?"

"Always. I took a look at the pictures. Heck of a lot of files. But I can make room for you over here at our IPS office."

Logan and Summer stopped at the entrance of the building and waited since AA meetings were usually closed to members. They had no desire to violate anyone's privacy. They only wanted information.

"Are you sure? I don't want to impose."

"Of course you do. That's why you called asking for a favor," Chance said, his tone lighthearted, and Logan chuckled.

The door of the auxiliary building swung open, and people began moseying out. Perfect timing.

Summer pulled someone off to the side and spoke to them.

"Do you and the lawyer need any help going through the files?" Chance asked. "And what's her name again?"

"Summer Stratton. And I'm sure any assistance you can provide would be appreciated. We're going to have our hands full looking into the death of Dani Granger and investigating Einhorn Industries." The two of them shouldn't have to sacrifice sleep to comb through boxes of information when Chance was gracious enough to offer help.

"Give me the address and we can pick everything up for you."

Logan rattled it off. "We're about to interview someone.

As soon as we're done, we'll leave the key under the mat by the front door. Should be there in less than an hour. Lock up when you're done and take it with you. We'll pick the key up at the office."

"Sounds good," Chance said. "See you later."

Logan hung up, putting away his phone, and turned to Summer as she thanked the woman she was speaking to and joined him.

"We want to talk to Mike Johnson," Summer said, and Logan was reminded how there was no such thing as anonymity in small towns. "Tall. Beard. Glasses. She said we can't miss him."

They headed inside.

Cleaning up a table lined with doughnuts, cookies and other refreshments, Mike was easy to spot. Several members chatted with him, and others stacked chairs.

"Excuse me," Summer said, drawing his attention as the conversation ended, "do you run the AA meetings?"

"Sure do. Well, most of them. I'm Mike." He offered them a pleasant smile that reached his eyes. "What can I do for you?"

The guy was taller and fitter than expected. Despite the short graying hair and silver-speckled beard, he didn't look older than his late forties.

Logan remembered seeing him at Dani's funeral, but they hadn't been introduced. Mike had clearly been grieving. On the verge of tears.

"I'm Summer Stratton and this is Logan Powell. I was Dani Granger's best friend and he was her cousin," she said, and recognition of the name dawned across Mike's face. "I'm the attorney who filed the lawsuit against Einhorn on Dani's behalf. Now we're looking into the events surrounding her death."

The man's smile faded as he nodded solemnly. "You were at the funeral, weren't you?" he asked Logan.

"Yes, I was." He shook Mike's offered hand. "But we didn't get a chance to speak."

"Dani talked about you, Summer, on more than one occasion. Very highly, I might add. I know you two were very close."

"I wish I could say the same, but she never mentioned you."

"That's the nature of AA," Mike said. "We keep this part of our lives separate from the rest unless we're making amends or asking a loved one to attend a milestone celebration. How can I be of help?"

"Can you tell us if Dani regularly attended meetings," Logan said, "and if so, did she miss any around the weeks leading up to her death?"

"Ask anyone here." Mike gestured to the handful of people still hovering nearby. "Dani attended a meeting every single week. Not always the same day and time. But she came here for AA even when there were Sundays she missed church service."

"I told you," Summer said, giving Logan a sexy, know-it-all look.

"Did Dani show any signs of depression? Stress?" Logan asked. "Any reason you think she might've been drinking the night of her alleged accident?"

"I was her sponsor." Mike pushed the sleeves of his Henley shirt up to his forearms and shoved his hands in his jean pockets. "When she was feeling low, she told me, so I could check in with her more frequently. That happened after her mom and later her dad passed away. But she always bounced back. Never had a relapse. Sobriety was a part of her everyday life. Right along with trying to prove that Einhorn was responsible for killing her cattle and for her father's death. Especially in the last four to six months. She became a woman on a mission. The news of what happened to her hit us all hard."

Summer stood a bit taller, confidence radiating from her. "Dani did talk about you, but not by name. I guess because it's AA. She told me that her sponsor gave the best hugs and that you were a great listener. That talking to you over a piece of pie was better than a drink ever was when she felt stressed."

Mike smiled but it was full of barely contained grief. "Thank you. For telling me that. It means a lot."

As much as Logan wanted to share in Summer's satisfaction that she was right about Dani's state of mind, Logan didn't want to jump to conclusions prematurely. "Did Dani's behavior change at all in the last few months or weeks?"

Mike considered the question for a moment. "Well, she did start acting a bit obsessive about Einhorn and kind of paranoid. Started talking about how someone was following her. I thought she was losing it, but then she called me scared one night. Claimed someone broke in and stole evidence she was collecting. I went by to take a look. Sure enough, somebody had painted the word *Stop* in big, red letters on her dining room wall and had cleaned out her garage. That sent her spiraling to a dark place."

"One of depression?" Logan wondered.

"More like desperation." Mike sighed. "Dani was willing to cross any line to get what she wanted."

Folding her arms, Summer narrowed her eyes. "What do you mean by that?"

Mike shrugged. "Dani blamed Einhorn for destroying her family's farm, for her father's cancer. She wanted proof they were responsible. I got the impression she'd do anything to get it."

"Even break the law?" Logan asked.

Summer gave him a pointed look. "Dani would never do that."

"I wouldn't be so sure." Mike looked around and lowered his voice. "Several months ago, Dani broke into Chip Boyd's place, convinced he was the one who took all her stuff, and stole his computer. Got someone to hack into it for her."

Logan glanced at the gawkers paying more attention to them than the refreshments or putting away chairs. "Are you talking about Charles Boyd, the deputy CSO over at Einhorn Industries?" he asked.

"One and the same, but he goes by Chip. The entire Einhorn security team is dodgy."

"But that doesn't sound like Dani." Summer shook her head. "She'd never break the law."

"Desperation can drive people to do unpredictable things they wouldn't normally consider," Mike said. "Even things that run counter to their morality."

Concern flared in her eyes as she pressed the heel of her hand to her forehead. "Do you know if she found anything on Boyd's laptop?"

"I don't think so, because she only spiraled harder after that," Mike said. "Things started heating up on all sides for her. I told her to leave it alone. But Dani was so headstrong, she wouldn't listen."

Nodding, Summer frowned. "The obstinate part sounds exactly like her."

"Other than the leadership at Einhorn," Logan said, thinking specifically about the security team, "is there anyone else in town who might've had cause to silence Dani?"

"Besides half the town in general, the only other person who comes to mind is Roy Nielsen."

"The name doesn't ring bell," Summer said. "What would be his motive?"

"Money. Plain and simple. Since the lawsuit was made public, Roy has made it known he's not too happy about it. Turns out he's a major shareholder in Einhorn Industries. Something like thirty to forty percent."

Fairly significant.

"Nielsen stands to lose a lot if the lawsuit doesn't go in Einhorn's favor," Mike added. "Ever since his son, RJ, Roy Jr., came back home, he's been a constant thorn in Dani's side."

"Came back from where?" Logan asked.

"The army. Did twelve years. Special Forces hotshot," Mike said with a deep undercurrent of disdain. "I hated the way he treated Dani."

An older woman with a weathered face and auburn hair pulled up in a tight bun had steadily edged down along the refreshment table, moving closer to them. Now she wasn't even trying to hide the fact that she was eavesdropping as she gave Mike a hard side-eye.

Mike must've sensed the woman staring, because he glanced over his shoulder at her. Then he quickly jerked his head back around like the sight of her standing within earshot scared him. He cleared his throat. "Just so there's no misunderstanding, I'm not accusing RJ or Einhorn of anything. I don't need any trouble."

Logan was used to small-town busybodies hungry for gossip, but it occurred to him that interviewing Mike here, with so many members still lurking, might've put him in danger. "Can we get your phone number in case we have any follow-up questions?"

"Sure," Mike said and gave it to them.

Summer entered the number in her phone. "Out of curiosity, when was the last time you saw Dani?"

"Three days before the accident. We celebrated her five-year sober anniversary, and I gave her the coin she had been eagerly waiting for. The big five, she called it. She was so happy. Proud. And she had every right to be. Hang on a second." Mike took out his cell, brought something up on the screen of his phone and showed it to them.

A picture of Mike standing next to Dani, his arm wrapped tight around her shoulder, hers curled around his waist, his cheek resting on the top of her head as she held up the coin that had a prominent number five in the center. Dani's brown eyes sparkled with pure joy. Her cheeks were flushed a rosy pink. She and Mike were both beaming.

"Between you and me," Mike said, his voice a sad whisper, "my guess is that Dani crossed the wrong line, with the wrong person, and it got her killed."

Logan intended to make sure the same thing didn't happen to Summer.

Chapter Nine

By four o'clock, they stood out on the broad porch of the Granger house while Special Agent Declan Hart finished collecting evidence inside.

Summer left the key to the rented cabin under the welcome mat for Chance Reyes before heading over to the house with Logan. She had already packed a bag earlier after Logan insisted that she couldn't be there alone. Although the cabin was cozy, with the best view in town, it was a little too cozy for two. It only had one bedroom and the *sofa* was little more than a love seat, not nearly long enough to comfortably accommodate Logan's long frame.

Standing on Dani's front porch, forced to stay in her house, all for protection from an unknown assailant who probably had also murdered her best friend, had pressure swelling in Summer's chest. Her mind kept spinning around all the things Mike had told them. Now she couldn't escape the memories, the grief, the strain of the lawsuit. Not even for an evening. Not stuck out here on the Grangers' land, where Dani had spent her last days. Terrified. Alone. Obsessed.

"Thinking about Dani?" Logan asked.

Always.

Summer looked over at him. Dark brown cowboy hat on

his head, a form-fitting white T-shirt that showed off his athletic physique, sculpted arms, broad shoulders and narrowed waist. The battered denim he had on emphasized his muscular legs. Scarred, sturdy work boots that matched his personality. Rancher's hands—strong, tanned, calloused. He was the type of good-looking that would make any woman take notice, more than once, but the best parts about him were more than skin-deep.

"The things Mike said about her." She shook her head, still trying to process everything, finding it hard to accept. "It didn't sound like the woman I knew. Breaking and entering. Stealing a computer."

Logan strode closer and put a hand on her shoulder. "She was desperate. Probably at her wits' end for closure after two years of fighting this battle."

Her heart sank, near breaking. "But I was fighting it with her." Putting everything on the line. "She wasn't in this alone."

"Maybe she still felt alone," Logan said, his voice soft and supportive in a see-both-sides kind of way. "Here. In Cutthroat Creek. Surrounded by vipers who wanted her to stop digging. Who were harassing and intimidating her. Sounds like it drove her to extreme measures."

She appreciated his empathy. As a lawyer, often working with the worst of the worst, it was a hard-to-come-by trait she highly valued. It had been a long time since she'd been around a man like him. Simple but not basic. Tough yet sweet. Ethical and good-hearted and so darn hot it was a distraction to be near him.

"Even if she had found something on Boyd's laptop," she said, "we would've had to tell the court how it was obtained. That's why I insisted that Jeff Arbuckle track everything Dani brought in. I didn't want any nasty surprises later on in court."

"Would it have been admissible since it's a civil lawsuit and not a criminal case?"

"The defense would've challenged any illegally obtained evidence. If the court allowed it to be introduced, Einhorn could use it as grounds for an appeal, not to mention how it would've exposed Dani to charges of theft and a potential lawsuit for damages." Doing the wrong thing for the right reasons still made it wrong. The ends didn't always justify the means.

"She probably didn't realize that. Or she didn't care, so long as she nailed Einhorn."

"Maybe it's my fault she took such drastic steps. I complained to her about spending sixteen hours a day going through the discovery files Einhorn had turned over and the pressure I was under at my firm. I didn't even tell everything. How bad it was getting for me. About taking two pay cuts because I wasn't bringing in new clients. I worried that I not only wasn't going to make partner like this, but might end up losing my job. Dani was used to me being the strong one who had it all together. I shouldn't have burdened her. But I was so frustrated trying to search for a needle in a haystack in the dark with just a flashlight. I told her that if only I knew what I was looking for, an email, a report, a test, something proving Einhorn Industries was aware of the chemicals in the fertilizer, the damage it could do, and simply didn't care that it would've been a hundred times easier to find it in the discovery." Tears stung Summer's eyes. She never should've dumped her stress onto Dani's shoulders when her friend was already under more than enough strain. "What if she was doing that? Taking a dangerous shortcut. Illegally looking for the smoking gun to steer my search through the files for legal evidence."

"You can't assume what she was thinking. It'll only torture you."

"But she did find something concrete." And it was probably hidden in that house somewhere. "I wish she had talked to me." Tears fell from her eyes and she quickly whisked them away, not wanting to break down in front of him or ruin her makeup. "Confided more. Trusted me."

Logan stepped forward and silently wrapped his arms around her in a hug. His embrace was warm and soothing. She sagged against him, resting her head on his shoulder, digging her fingers into his muscled arms, and his reassuring presence closed more tightly around her.

Poor Dani. Only twenty-eight. Never had a chance to become a veterinarian the way she'd planned. To fall in love. To get married. Start the family she had wanted.

Her death filled Summer with a nasty mix of guilt, grief, deep regret and anger that Dani's shining light in the world had been extinguished.

Life is fragile and so very short.

"Dani loved you," he said. "She did trust you and confided in you. But she probably knew that you would've told her not to take the last-ditch measures she was set on. I'm sure Dani didn't want to show you that side of her because she didn't want to disappoint you."

He couldn't possibly know that. Summer pulled back from him. "Those are pretty big assumptions. You barely knew Dani."

"But I think I've got a fairly good read on you. Easy to love. Loyal to the point that you're risking your job. Sacrificing salary. All to help your best friend. You have high standards, Summer Stratton, which is good, but with those come equally high expectations. For yourself as well as for others. If *I'm* worried about disappointing you, I'd say it's safe to assume so was Dani."

His words stroked over her senses, leaving her heart aching and tender. Stunned by his razor-sharp assessment, blown away that he was worried about disappointing her when she was merely grateful to have him here, she stared at him.

At his warm blue eyes. At his chiseled features.

Logan brushed hair back from her face, his calloused fingers caressing her cheek, gentle and featherlight, but also weighty. A sad smile tugged at his mouth and the way his lips curved sparked a deep yearning that spread all the way through her stomach. To know what his lips would feel like pressed to hers.

His cell phone chimed. He dropped his hand, reaching into his pocket. Taking out the phone, he looked at the screen. "Chance has all the boxes loaded and is hauling them back to the IPS office."

"Already? That was fast for one man. There are fifty heavy boxes." Her back protested every time she moved one.

"Well, he does have three guys helping him."

"What exactly does Ironside Protection Services do?" Summer asked, needing the conversation to focus on something other than how she might've driven her best friend to reckless actions. "Are they bodyguards for hire?"

"They can be if necessary. Depends on what the client needs. IPS employs a lot of ex-military. Chance being an exception because of his legal expertise. But they offer security services that run the gamut from protection details to risk management and all sorts of investigative and intelligence work."

"If that's the case, then why didn't you or Ric ask Chance to look into Dani's death with me instead of coming all the way out here yourself?"

His lips twisted in a lopsided grin. "Sick of me already?"

Smiling, she stepped closer into his personal space, testing the boundary between them. Instead of moving away, he leaned in.

"Not at all," she said. "I wasn't complaining. Only curious."

"Ric wanted family to handle it since Dani was his niece. He thought someone in law enforcement would be better suited than him to do it."

"You mentioned that you two aren't close. Why not?" Dani never really talked about her extended family and Summer never had a reason to ask. "Doesn't he live on the ranch with you and the other Powells?"

Logan lowered his gaze like he didn't want to discuss it.

"I'm sorry if I'm prying. You don't have to tell me." She rocked back on her heels, giving him room to breathe. "I didn't mean to overstep."

He caught her wrist and tugged her back toward him. "You didn't. I promised to tell you and I'm a man of my word," he said, his thumb stroking her arm.

The topic was clearly a difficult one. After her summers at her cousins' ranch, she had witnessed plenty of family drama. More than enough to understand the discomfort that could come from explanations. "Doesn't mean you have to do it now."

"Won't get any easier later." He glanced out at the land. "Matt's mother, Ric's wife, Ivy, ran off with another man when Matt was little, leaving their family to deal with her gambling debts. Ivy is my mom's twin sister," he said, and she stiffened at the surprising news. "Not only did Ric show up at our ranch in dire financial straits, hat in hand needing a job, but then, every single day, he was forced to look at a carbon copy of the woman who'd skipped out on him. On the outside, my mom, Holly, and Ivy are identical except for how they wear their hair. But in all the other ways that matter, they're polar opposites. Ric steered Matt toward us, asked for him to live in the main house, while my uncle stayed in the bunkhouse with the other ranch hands. There's always been this weird distance between us. I could never fully grasp the difficulty of Uncle Ric's position. Although now I think I understand it much better than when I was a kid."

"Complicated is an understatement." Summer imagined what it must've been like for Ric, jagged claws sinking into his chest every time he set eyes on Holly, seeing the face of the woman who'd walked away with another man, abandoned their child and left him with her gambling debts to boot. The man must've been truly destitute to swallow his pride and turn to his sister-in-law for help. "Good parents make extraordinary sacrifices for the sake of their children. To give them a better life."

Her parents had taken out a second mortgage on their house to pay for Autumn's doctorate degree and used what they had left to help put Summer through law school.

"Matt grew up wanting for nothing," Logan said, "but ironically resenting everything."

As tough as the situation must've been for Ric, it must have been just as confusing and hard for Matt. "It was still really nice of you to unburden Matt, let him enjoy his vacation and come out here to help. Very generous."

He looked up at her. "If I'm being completely honest, I didn't do it just for him. I wanted—"

"I think I've got everything I need," Special Agent Declan Hart said, stepping out of the house, wearing latex gloves and carrying sealed evidence bags.

Logan let go of her wrist and swung around to face the other man.

Declan strode closer, authority radiating off the Montana agent like sunbeams, the antithesis to Sheriff Tofteland. Declan was a handsome man. Rich brown skin smoother than mahogany, soulful brown eyes, a trim mustache. Six feet tall and buff, he wore a mint green polo shirt tucked into jeans that had nary a wrinkle, and a cream-colored cowboy hat. He was both polished and rugged at the same time. Bad-boy swagger packaged with good-guy vibes. A dichotomy she found bothersome, but one that she was certain her sister Autumn would've been drawn to.

"I'd say I'm shocked the sheriff didn't come out to do this," Declan said, "but I've had some dealings with Tofteland." He pulled off the latex gloves. "You think the attack is related to the death of Dani Granger?"

"We do," Logan said.

"I'm certain of it," Summer said. "We have strong reason to believe that she wasn't drinking that night and the car crash was no accident like the coroner declared."

"In the past twenty-five years, since Genburg has been the county coroner and Tofteland the sheriff, you know how many autopsies Genburg has requested the medical examiners perform?"

Neither Summer nor Logan ventured a guess.

"Five," Declan said, providing the answer.

"What?" Logan sounded aghast. "You can't be serious."

"Unfortunately, I am. From what I can tell, Genburg tends to rubber-stamp the death certificates based on Sheriff Tofteland's findings." Declan sighed. "Are you Dani Granger's next of kin?" he asked Logan.

"No. My uncle is."

"If you can get a power of attorney, we can exhume the body and request an autopsy from the medical examiners who work for the state. That would be faster and easier than trying to get a warrant to make it happen."

"I have power of attorney. Summer recommended that my uncle get one for whichever relative was going to come out here to look into Dani's death," Logan said, stroking her arm.

Only doing her due diligence after face time with Sheriff Tofteland and him issuing a warning to have her arrested for trespassing.

Declan glanced at the point of contact between her and Logan. His look was direct, penetrating. She guessed that he didn't miss much.

"Smart to get the power of attorney," Declan said. "Let's use it. I can call in a favor with the forensic science division. They're only two floors above me. I can have the body exhumed tomorrow and ask them to expedite *everything*." He held up the bags of evidence and shook them.

Finally, the wheels of progress were turning after being stalled for weeks.

"Since we think the lawsuit that Summer and Dani filed against Einhorn Industries is related to all this," Logan said, "we're going to go over there and question a couple of people on their security team. Emma Einhorn and Chip Boyd. Though any of them could be behind it. Any interest in coming along?"

Declan frowned. "I'd say my presence is a necessity. Otherwise, they'll simply stonewall you. The Einhorns are used to doing what they want when they want. Trying to go about this on your own is not the way. I'm the only one with real authority here. Maybe take a step back from this and let me do my job."

"I came here to investigate," Logan said. "*With her. We intend to do so.*"

She had to admire Logan's determination to keep his word and not simply hand things off to Declan Hart. "Just as any private investigators would," she added.

"But we'd rather do it with you," Logan said, tagging back in. "I want and requested Montana DCI's involvement. But not your hindrance."

Declan seemed to weigh their words. "I get it. If I were in your shoes, operating in someone else's jurisdiction, carrying a meaningless badge for all intents and purposes, I'd feel the same. I don't do powerless very well either."

The tension in Logan's shoulders eased and his brow smoothed out. "Thank you."

"Roy Nielsen and his son, RJ, are also on our list of people to talk to," Summer said. "Do you know them?"

Declan shook his head. "Not personally. I've never had any interaction with either, but the name Nielsen is well-known around these parts. RJ is a bit of a local celebrity for all the wrong reasons, if you ask me. He was in the Special Forces. Came home with the Distinguished Service Cross for heroism. Can't stop bragging about how many people he killed. Also, all the Nielsen farming equipment stores in the state belong to his family. His father has deep pockets."

"Roy Nielsen is also a major shareholder of Einhorn Industries," Logan said.

"The plot thickens." Declan grimaced. "When questioning the Einhorns and Nielsens, we need to tread lightly. What we don't want is for them to lawyer up and pipe down. With the assault against the two of you last night, I understand this is personal for you."

"The murder of my best friend makes this personal," Summer clarified.

Declan took a deep breath, and she could tell he was trying to handle this delicately. "If you're too close to the situation to remove emotion," he said, "then it would be best for me talk to them alone."

No way were they going to be sidelined. "Logan and I are capable of being professionals about this." He was a DCI special agent and she was chief counsel for the lawsuit against Einhorn. "Emotion won't cloud our judgment or get in the way." That was more of a hope than a guarantee. The people in Cutthroat Creek had a way of getting under her skin.

Declan gave a curt nod, then looked at Logan.

"You heard the lady."

"All right. But bear in mind that we are not approaching this as a team effort. I'm allowing you both to accompany me as a professional courtesy only," Declan said, his face serious as he studied them. "Got it?"

Not a team?

They'd found these leads, which they didn't have to share and could've pursued on their own.

But Declan was the one with the badge and legitimate authority, she reminded herself. They needed to do this by the book. Once they found Dani's killer and whoever had attacked them, Summer didn't want the person getting off on a technicality because they had gone rogue.

Work the system. If she did as she'd been taught, there wouldn't be any risk of a miscarriage of justice. She needed to do this the right way, for Dani.

Logan glanced at her.

Summer nodded. "Yes, understood," she said to Declan, speaking for them both.

"Let me get a photo of your power of attorney for the paperwork to have Ms. Granger's body exhumed. Hopefully, first thing in the morning. The sooner we get the autopsy done, the better. I'll make it my top priority and get the ball rolling on that and ballistics. In the morning, I'll give you a call, letting you know what time to meet me at Einhorn Industries." Declan handed her a business card. "My personal cell is written on the back. Logan, you already have my number," he said, and she recalled the text message Declan had sent Logan. "Now, I want you two to tell me everything you know about this case, so we're on the same page. No detail is too small. Don't leave anything out."

Summer took comfort in having another ally in this. She and Logan might not be leading this investigation anymore, but they weren't stuck on the sidelines, watching from the bench. They were on the field, in the game. Exactly where she preferred to be.

Chapter Ten

Logan drove through Bitterroot Falls, the town on the other side of the lake, heading to IPS.

"It's generous of Chance to give up space at his office to store all those files," Summer said, seated in the passenger's seat. "Not to mention the manual labor of hauling everything over."

Logan couldn't agree more. "Yeah, I owe him for this."

Asking for a favor was new territory for Logan. He was usually the one always ready to oblige. Ready to put his own wants and needs on the back burner. Never leaning on others. Never thinking twice about helping out family or a friend.

Though, in this case, he considered Chance Reyes to be both.

The Powell and Reyes families were meant to be joined through marriage. Once upon a time, Logan had assumed he'd be the one to marry Amber. A silly teenage fantasy that had distorted his judgment, obscuring the reality that he had only been an afterthought for her. Someone who might've been her second choice if fate hadn't stepped in, saving them both from settling for less than they deserved.

He had no regrets. The experience had taught him what he was really looking for, what he needed in a partner. And through it, the years he'd spent watching out for Amber and never being the one in his family to hurt her—when his parents and Monty had, all in a complicated, manipulative effort to get the Reyes land—he and Chance had formed a unique bond. A close friendship that couldn't be fully defined. Or broken.

Logan was the brother Chance never had.

And Chance was the buddy Logan never had in his own brothers.

"Thank you for going out of your way to help me like this." Summer's smile was sad around the edges. "I know it's not what you signed up for when you agreed to come here. After dealing with that rattlesnake, you probably wish your brother Jackson had been available instead."

Not for a second. "I like the unexpected. Keeps me on my toes," he said, and this time the smile reached her eyes. He was also glad that he was getting to know Summer better and spend time with her, as he'd hoped.

"Sorry you have to play babysitter. I'm sure I'd be fine in a big hotel with security cameras in Kalispell or Missoula."

He could use a security system at the house, as well as better locks. "Both are an hour away." One to the north, the other to the south. "Besides the expense, it's an unnecessary inconvenience. Also, hotels tend to give people a false sense of security. That guy could grab a maid's universal room key, slip inside and wait for you. Or knock on your door, pretending to be hotel security. Once you open up, all he has to do is shove his way inside."

She frowned. "That's grim."

"That's reality. Staying in a hotel also won't stop someone from tampering with your car, like cutting your brakes," he said, putting on his blinker. He made a left turn at the light and parked in front of the office of Ironside Protection Services. "Or putting something worse than a rattler inside."

"What's worse than a rattlesnake?"

"That you wouldn't see or expect?" He shrugged and put his arm on the console, angling toward her. "Off the top of my head, a black widow. Their venom is fifteen times more potent than a rattler's."

Summer shivered, rubbing her hands over her arms. "I'd rather avoid both."

"I guess we have to stick together. In the interest of mutual safety."

"I guess so."

"Think of me as your bodyguard. Here to serve and protect, and the best way for me to do that is to keep you close." The task his uncle had asked of him was to investigate, but the primary mission had become keeping her safe, and that was everything. "If you can put up with me."

"I think I can manage the hardship." She grinned. "Seriously, you're the one making the real sacrifice, putting yourself in harm's way by helping me." She reached over and took his hand. "Thank you," she said, giving it a half shake and a half squeeze.

The gesture was friendly and warm, but she didn't let go.

"It's not a sacrifice," he said. "I want to be here. Doing this. For Dani. My uncle. *For you.*" He felt good in her presence, being near her. Seen and appreciated. More alive and awake than he had in months, and it had nothing to do with the danger and everything to do with her.

They stared at each other for a long while, her hand lingering in his. He couldn't bring himself to break the silence or to let her go. Then she chewed on her bottom lip with a look in her eye, a mix of nerves and possibly heat, and he wanted to bring her closer and kiss her.

"I've been thinking about the lawsuit," she finally said.

"Not about dropping it, I hope," he said, tightening his fingers around hers.

"No. Never. Just that I need to warn the other farmers who are plaintiffs. They've heard about Dani and soon they'll know about Jeff, if they don't already. I need to tell them to keep a low profile. Better yet, to get out of town for a while."

"If they are anything like the ranchers back home, they won't be inclined to leave their land and go into hiding."

"No, they won't, but I also need to make sure nothing happens to them. Too many lives have already been lost. My conscience can't handle another."

"We'll figure something out," he said, lifting his left hand to her face, and caressed her cheek. Continued to stare into her eyes. "Maybe they can be persuaded to take a vacation."

"I hope so." Her voice was soft, her eyes searching his.

He leaned in, slowly, testing the boundary.

A car horn beeped beside them, making them jerk apart.

HEART THUDDING, Summer looked around, annoyed at the jarring disruption. The loud, short noise was the sound of someone ensuring their vehicle was locked.

A man stood in the IPS office window, holding up a key fob, watching them. Smiling, he waved.

"That's Chance Reyes," Logan said with a grin. "We should go in."

"Yeah." She nodded, wishing they were back in that little bubble where nothing and no one else existed and he was about to kiss her.

They exited the vehicle. Logan held the door open for her and they entered the air-conditioned building.

"You could've given us a minute," Logan said, hugging Chance.

A mischievous smile curled on Chance's mouth as they pulled out of the embrace. "I was generous and gave you ten. You're welcome."

He'd been watching them the entire time?

"Thanks for all your help," Logan said.

"Anything for you, brother. All you have to do is ask, and if it's within my power to give, you shall receive."

Strong words. For some reason, he seemed like the kind of guy who would back it up with action.

"This is Summer Stratton," Logan said, turning to her.

"A pleasure to meet you." Chance shook her hand.

His grip was a little too strong, but the smile offset it.

"Trust me," she said, "the pleasure is all mine. I really appreciate your assistance."

"We both appreciate it," Logan added.

"No problem at all. I only wish you had given me a heads-up you were going to be in my neck of the woods. Especially if it was to *unleash chaos*." Chance's mouth quirked again. "No fair you have all the fun, not bothering to invite me to the party."

The man was tall, tanned and, in a word, debonair. It wasn't simply the luxury watch on his wrist, the handcrafted Lucchese boots—she'd been given a pair as a law school graduation gift, they stood out—or the tailored shirt that fit him like a glove.

She got the impression that he would somehow look suave wearing a burlap sack.

"This party has been deadly," Logan said. "Not quite what I was expecting. I didn't intend to rope you into this at all."

"The road to hell is paved with good intentions. I prefer transparency," Chance quipped back, amusement on his face. "Speaking of deadly, can we help on the security side of things?"

"It's not safe for Summer to stay at the place she rented by herself, so we'll be at Dani Granger's house together," Logan said, and Chance gave them a coy smirk that made Summer squirm. "I'm going to buy new locks for the house, but the place will still be vulnerable. You don't happen to have a high-tech security system that I can install tonight, do you?"

"We have something you could use. Not the level of security you probably want, but we can set up a few cameras to cover blind spots for you. I'll have one of the guys install them today."

"Give me the system, instructions, and I can do it," Logan said.

"This is our bread and butter. We can have it taken care of in under an hour. No instructions necessary." Chance patted him on the shoulder. "I'll show you where we set up the files. This way." He led them through the one-story building to a large conference room in the back. Boxes were lined up in stacks around the perimeter of the room, and three other men were inside, sitting at the table. "This is the motley crew. That's Bo Lennox, Tak Yazzie and Eli Easton," he said, tossing out introductions. A diverse bunch. "Logan Powell, brother from another mother, and Summer Stratton, attorney brave enough to go up against Einhorn Industries."

They exchanged handshakes and made a little small talk.

"I hate to impose on you like this. Won't you need the space in here for meetings?" Summer asked. "Or for briefing your staff?"

"Staff." Bo chuckled, leaning back in his seat and putting his feet up on a nearby chair.

"We prefer team," Chance said. "I may technically be in charge of the office, but we all work together. As for meetings, we can hold them in one of our offices. Trust me, this is not an imposition." He turned to the boxes. "Your discovery process has proven fruitful. Einhorn sent you the whole kit and caboodle in response to your RFP."

A request for production of documents could include almost anything. Contracts, emails, medical records, lab tests, financial statements, maintenance logs, photos—all discoverable when relevant.

"They're trying to bury me in it," she said. "I found Christmas cards dated ten years back, recipes, notes about what color to make the packaging of their products. Garbage to waste my time."

Chance shrugged, appearing unfazed. "That's the nature of the beast, is it not?"

Her own firm had used the very same tactic numerous times when defending corporations such as Einhorn. "It is, but being on the receiving end sucks."

"The boxes you have marked as reviewed are on this side." Chance gestured to the right. "The rest far outnumber the others."

She stared at the daunting stacks. "I've been going through them all by myself." Normally, she had a team of paralegals assisting her.

"Aren't you working with a local attorney on the lawsuit?" Chance asked.

"I was, with Jeff Arbuckle." Which reminded her that she needed to contact his assistant to get into his office and collect everything he had regarding the lawsuit.

"He's dead," Logan said. "Drowned in an alleged boating accident."

Eli leaned forward in his seat, resting his arms on the table. "I read about that this morning in the *Beacon*. Didn't realize he was a lawyer attached to the same case as Dani Granger. It wasn't mentioned in the paper."

"Summer was also attacked," Logan said, "shot." He gestured to the bandage on her arm. "And someone put a rattler in her car."

Tak sucked air through his teeth with a hiss. "Nasty business, rattlers."

"Hence the urgency of the message I left you," Logan said.

Chance sighed. "You skipped a few important details."

"Someone wants this lawsuit to disappear and they're tying up loose ends by making the deaths look like accidents." Logan turned to Summer, concern heavy in his eyes. "I'm going to make sure she stays safe." He spoke to the room, his gaze never leaving hers.

But she wasn't the only one in danger. "There are four other farmers as plaintiffs. We need to give them a heads-up about what's going on."

"Hold on." Bo put his feet on the floor and sat up. "If whoever is behind this wants it to look like everyone had an accident, why shoot her?"

"I don't think he meant to," Logan said. "The guy blocked the back door, leaving the front door clear. I believe he shot at her to force her to run to her car where the rattlesnake was waiting. He grazed her by accident."

"Was Dani Granger the kind of person to be easily intimidated or to take a bribe to back off?" Tak asked.

"No." Summer shook her head. "Never."

"Three accidents might be plausible," Tak said, moving his head from side to side as though he was thinking it through. "But not seven, and surely, these farmers have families. Bodies start piling up and a deadly cover-up becomes obvious. To everyone. With Granger, Arbuckle and you dead, the other farmers could be pressured into accepting a small settlement to leave it alone."

Chance rubbed his clean-shaven jaw. "I was going to ask how we could help further, but I think I know how. Give us a list of the farmers and we'll reach out to them to let them know about the potential danger. Just in case. Summer, you need a local attorney attached to your lawsuit. Use me until you find someone else better suited to avoid any unnecessary delays in the lawsuit. As for this heap of discovery, tell us what you're looking for in all these boxes and we'll pitch in."

"Oh, I can't ask you do that." Summer glanced around the room at the eager faces.

"You didn't." Chance grinned. "I offered and if you're worried about our expertise, let me set your mind at ease. I've been practicing law for a decade and these fellas are some of the best investigators you'll ever come across. Bloodhounds. Give them a whiff of what you're looking for and once they've got the scent, they'll find it."

Smooth talker. Persuasive, too.

Logan was already doing so much when he barely knew Dani, wasn't even close to his uncle, and owed Summer nothing.

Now, through extension of him, four more were going to step in to help her when they owed her absolutely nothing either.

"I can see the apprehension written all over your face. For a bigwig attorney you're not very good at hiding your emotions," Chance said, the insult pulling her from her thoughts. "How well does that work for you in court?"

She reminded herself to breathe.

Chance Reyes was a lot to take in.

Too much.

"In the courtroom, I use a persona," she said without thinking, letting one of her secrets slip. It was all about preparation and acting.

"An alter ego?" Chance asked, grinning. "Like Sasha Fierce?"

"Not quite." Summer was no megastar Beyoncé with a powerful alter ego such as Sasha Fierce, capable of captivating sold out arenas.

"Give us a minute," Logan said, putting a hand on her shoulder. "To talk about it."

"Only to talk?" Chance raised an eyebrow. "If so, you can use my office across the hall. But if you were interested in finishing what you started while parked out front, it might require a different kind of room."

Way. Too. Much.

"The hall is fine." Logan ushered her out of the room, closed the door and steered her a few feet away from the conference room. "What's your concern?"

"The use of their time." In her world, time was money. Billable hours were everything. They reigned supreme. She'd had none for almost a year, was burning through vacation days out here, and was about to lose her job because of it all unless she managed to get a huge settlement from this lawsuit. "They must have other things to work on."

"How long would it take you and me to finish going through the rest of those boxes, after a full day of investigating, at night, when we're not sleeping."

She shrugged. "Months."

"Exactly. With the four of them working on it full-time, they could get it done in weeks. Possibly days. Using them frees us up to focus on what really happened to Dani and Arbuckle and find out who is after you."

"But…but I can't pay them what their time would be worth."

He clutched her shoulders, drawing closer. "You're not coming out of pocket for this, and it's not like they get paid by the hour anyway. They're salaried. If they weren't available to help, believe me, Chance would not have offered. In fact, they just wrapped up a couple of cases. IPS is going to pay those guys whether they're working on this or not."

"What if they had planned to take time off? Relax. Recharge."

"That's not how they're wired. Especially with two people dead and you under fire."

She had no clue how they were wired, but they were still people with lives and needs beyond work. On the other hand, what he said made sense about allowing them to sort through the documents to save precious time that was running out, but… "I feel bad."

"We need help. You need help. How much sleep have you been getting?"

"Not much. Usually four hours." If she was lucky. She was making do, testing her limits, on the brink of exhaustion nearly every day. But long hours without complaint was her norm.

"It's unsustainable. We need to be well-rested. Focused. Situational awareness plummets when someone is exhausted, and we can't afford that. Not in Cutthroat Creek, when we don't know exactly what we're up against. I'll be damned if I'm going to let something happen to you because we're spreading ourselves too thin."

Putting her hands on his chest, she leaned against him. "I'm so used to being independent, doing everything for myself, it's sometimes hard to let others step in without feeling beholden."

"What about with me?" He cupped the back of her neck, caressed her cheek with his thumb, stirring tingles low in her belly.

She looked into his eyes, so very blue and bright, and the rest of the world faded away. There was only him and her and this feeling she couldn't explain. "You're different."

"How?"

He wasn't simply giving his time and expertise when he didn't have to. He was standing by her, standing *with her* through this, risking his life. And not once had he made her feel indebted.

But he did make her *feel*. Emotions, sensations, desires she was struggling to rein in.

"If I owe you," she said, "then I need time to pay you back." Time for this. To know more about him. To touch him. To explore this yearning for more with him.

"I like the idea of collecting." His thumb brushed her bottom lip, sending a quiver through her. "Slowly."

Then what?

They'd each go back home to their respective lives, a thousand miles apart. And they would never see each other again.

A strange panic settled over her. An overwhelming, rattled sensation. She wasn't dating Logan, hadn't kissed him, and yet, the thought of never doing either sent a surge of nausea through her. Even worse, the idea of doing more than kissing—much, much more—and then not being with him after made her physically ill.

Someone cleared their throat, loudly, deliberately, and they both looked down the hall.

"I'd say a different kind of room is definitely required." Chance flashed a sly grin, and she pulled away from Logan as heat rushed over her face. "What's it going to be? The choice seems rather simple to me, but it is your choice."

Logan stared down at her.

No denying it, she needed more help. How could she refuse when there was so much at stake?

Summer shook off her embarrassment, headed back down the hall to the conference with Logan and faced everyone. "I'll walk you all through the case, show you what I have so far, go over what I hope to find in those boxes and explain why I may need to expand the lawsuit."

"Expand it how?" Tak asked.

"The contaminated creek that runs through Dani Granger's property feeds into the Bigfork River. It's likely that the people on the reservation are being poisoned."

"Sounds like we're in for a long night," Chance said.

"We'll need takeout." Bo stood. "I'll grab the menus."

Summer marveled at them. Their efficiency. Their dedication. All without complaint. "You're going above and beyond. Thank you so much." She turned to Logan, gave his arm a squeeze and mouthed another *Thank you*. If not for him, none of this would be happening. Montana DCI's involvement. Ironside Protection Services' assistance. Security cameras for the house. Logan was amazing.

"All right," Chance said, waving a dismissive hand at her. "Enough of that. Let's get to work."

Chapter Eleven

Even though it was late, Bo was kind enough to come out to the house and install the security cameras after Summer had finished explaining the particulars of the lawsuit to the IPS team. With Logan assisting and learning, Bo put up four cameras on the outside of the house, covering the doors and most of the exterior, but there were still a few troubling blind spots. While Bo checked the system and set up the tablet that could be used to monitor everything, Logan installed two more cameras inside the house.

People with nefarious intentions might spot the exterior cameras anyway and maneuver to avoid them. But almost no one would expect security cameras inside of an old farmhouse. One he positioned in a corner in the living room, to overlook the windows of the dining room and the window above the kitchen sink, where Summer had tried to escape. The last camera he placed to cover the foyer as well as the bottom of the stairs. In the event someone made it inside the house and attempted to sneak upstairs, he'd see them coming and it would give them a fighting chance.

"You're all set," Bo said, handing him a smart tablet that would enable Logan to keep an eye on things at all times. "Give me your cell phone. I'll download and sync the app for you."

Logan passed it to him. "Chance mentioned that you guys are all veterans."

"Yep. Prior US Air Force. Eli, Tak and I served together. Chance recruited us at our last duty station. The 819th RED HORSE Squadron at Malmstrom Air Force Base. That cunning devil knew exactly what he was doing. He'd just opened the IPS office. The owner, Rip Lockwood, had offered him a modest bonus for recruitment with double the money if he got vets to join, since Lockwood is a veteran himself. Chance scooped us out somehow, specifically eyeing people from RED HORSE. He was up-front. Told us that he'd cut us a generous percentage of his bonus as a new hire incentive. Chance got the three of us in one fell swoop, making IPS history to be the fastest to fully staff an office with all vets."

"That's Chance for you," Logan said, with a chuckle. "I've heard about RED HORSE." Rapid Engineer Deployable, Heavy Operational Repair Squadron Engineer. Always wartime-ready, they rapidly mobilized people, equipment, and provided heavy repair capability, construction support and combat engineering anywhere in the world. "My cousin Matt talked about how your squadron was critical during one of his missions for aircraft recovery and engineering support for some weapon systems."

"Your cousin must be Special Forces."

"As a matter of fact, he was."

"Those guys are the only ones who ever talk about us."

"Was the transition to IPS hard?" Logan wondered.

"Making the switch to civilian life was. We're used to being ready to deploy at a moment's notice. Doing sixteen-, sometimes twenty-hour, days under pressure, indefinitely. As engineers, we're used to investigating problems. Working a case is fairly similar. Out in the field, we had to take care of our own security, even in war zones. So, we're capable of handling ourselves, protecting people and infrastructure. The rest we've picked up along the way." Bo gave him back his phone. "You're good to go. There's a five-minute tutorial that'll walk you through the features."

"Appreciate you taking the time to do this."

They shook hands.

"No problem," Bo said. "Have a good night."

Logan let him out. Locking the door, he chided himself for not getting a new dead bolt yet. *Tomorrow.*

Every time he thought about tomorrow, conducting this investigation alongside Summer, unease threaded through him. She was already the target of an attack. Thrusting her further in the spotlight, having her front and center as they questioned people, might make matters worse.

Not that she was going to back down, even if he asked her to.

He walked through the living room, Summer had tidied up while he and Bo were installing the security cameras. He found her in the kitchen, working her way through the pantry, checking boxes and cleaning out cabinets. "Hey, I thought we agreed to search the house tomorrow, for whatever Dani might have hidden." In the daylight, when they were fresh.

"We did, but this still has to be done." She gestured to the cabinet full of spices and the essentials in the pantry that would never be used. "I'm already in cleaning mode. I figured we could at least get through the kitchen. Comb through it while cleaning it out. Scratch one room off the list."

Wearily, he nodded. "All right." He went over to the radio on the counter, flicked it on and scanned for a good station. "Always easier to do something when you're doing it with music."

IT WAS ALMOST MIDNIGHT, and fatigue crept through her. The day had been never-ending. Listening to the radio while they worked made the task far less dreary and tedious. But something weighed on Logan. He was too quiet, too stiff.

Summer helped him carry the last of the filled garbage bags to the trash bins outside. They passed the five-hundred-gallon propane tank that kept the hot-water heater, stove, dryer and refrigerator running. An essential in some parts of Montana, especially in the colder months. Light from the kitchen window provided enough illumination for them to see clearly. Music wafted out through the open door, carrying a sultry tune.

He dumped the last bag and turned back to the house.

"What's wrong?" she asked, stopping him.

"I'm tired."

She searched his face. "Is that all?"

He didn't answer, only nodded.

Her throat grew tight with nerves, and she swallowed against it. "I feel like you're holding something back from me. If you are, you can tell. I don't want secrets between us. Whatever it is I can handle it. Promise."

He grimaced. "I worried going forward with this investigation, with you, might be a mistake," he said and hesitated.

"Why?" She stared at him, waiting for him to explain. Not wanting to push him or hurry him.

"Letting you come to Einhorn Industries to speak with the security team will only expose you further. It might reinforce some sicko's idea that you're a problem. The more I turn it over in my head, the more it worries me that it might make things worse. Maybe you should spend the day at IPS and focus on the lawsuit. Let me and Declan poke around. Draw the town's ire away from you."

"Don't you see, the lawsuit is the problem." She ran her

palm against his sandpapery cheek, over the day's stubble. "What do you think I've been doing for the last two weeks? Sitting in that cabin under wraps, not daring to question anyone or show my face in public, too scared to announce who I am and why I am here? Everyone in Cutthroat Creek already knows that I'm a threat. The only way I'll stop asking questions about Dani, and now Jeff, or drop the lawsuit is if they kill me."

He clutched her arms and tugged her closer until her chest pressed to his. "I won't let that happen."

"I know." She slid her hand up his shoulder, to his neck and into his hair. "And tomorrow, they all know it, too. This is progress. Not potential failure. You are not endangering me by *letting* me come. Not that you can stop me," she said, and that brought a grin to his face. "We're going to show them that no matter what they do, I won't back down and I'm no longer alone."

"They'll have to come through me to get to you."

She believed him. With every fiber of her being.

He reached up and cupped her cheek, brushed his thumb across her bottom lip. Her breath caught in her throat, pulse fluttering unsteadily through her veins.

Every particle around them ionized.

"I like you, Summer. More than I've liked anyone in a really long time. I care about you," he said. "I'm attracted to you."

Holding her breath, unable to speak, she nodded.

Me, too.

"I wish tragedy wasn't bringing us together again," he said. "I wish that I had asked for your phone number that afternoon when we spoke outside on the porch."

Me, too. "It was a funeral. Probably would've been weird if you had." Weird but in a good way.

"I wish *this* was happening under normal circumstances."

"What would that normal look like?"

"I'd ask you out. Take you to dinner. Someplace with great food. On the water. Eat while the sun is setting. Maybe have a little wine."

Sounded like a perfect start. "And then?"

"We'd go dancing."

He wrapped his arm around her waist, and they swayed to the slow music coming from inside the house. She slid her arm over his shoulder and curled her hand on the back of his neck.

A slight breeze blew, rattling the branches of a nearby tree. She shivered, but not from the cold, and pressed her body even closer to his. He looked down into her eyes and she discovered an awareness that matched her own.

Electricity and heat flared between them.

And she wanted to feel more. To feel everything.

As they moved together to the music in perfect step, in complete harmony, alarm bells rang in her head. Warning her to stop. Demanding that she use caution.

But she didn't listen. Because she didn't want to.

Life was too fragile, too darn short not to take the smallest of risks. What she wanted was to know what it would be like to kiss him. Just once.

She glanced at his mouth, swallowed her nerves and rose up on her toes. But he angled his face away, lowering his head while keeping his arm snug around her.

His breath feathered over her neck, and her whole body tingled, coming alive. His lips brushed her jaw, then higher on her cheek—like he was giving her time to reconsider, a chance to run—and finally he kissed her. She sighed softly with longing, and his tongue answered, gliding into her mouth. She tasted him, savored the feel, the flavor, shivers spreading over her.

The kiss was sweet and slow and tentative.

But also, something deeper.

Something softer.

Something so much more profound. Unlike any other connection she'd had.

Because Logan was the one kissing her. This man, who'd chosen to make her fight his, risking his life, vowing to protect her, was the one holding her, touching her.

She closed her eyes and relished every second, memorized the feel of his lips against hers, his hands on her body, his breath flowing and mingling with hers. He angled his mouth across hers, and she opened willingly, tangling her tongue with his, reveling in this moment.

They swayed to the music and shared their breath and heat and presence. His arms tightened around her, his palm sliding lower. A small groan tore from his throat, and she wanted to cling to him. Wanted to feel his hands and mouth everywhere.

His other palm made its way to her breast, molding the cotton of her top and the lace of her bra over her flesh.

Warmth, heat and desire fired through her body, hot enough to reduce her to a pile of ash right where she stood.

Wake up! You live in Washington, and he lives in Wyoming, a thousand miles apart, the cold logical voice in her head pointed out. *This is a reckless moment in time, nothing more.*

This can be nothing more.

Reality hit her like a bucket of ice water, and the romantic mental cocoon shattered. She pulled away. "I like you, Logan. The attraction is mutual, but I'm…" Her voice trailed off as she wondered whether or not to tell him she was a virgin. "I'm not interested in a casual hookup."

He blinked several times, the image of innocent confusion. "Neither am I."

Then what were they doing?

"I know this has been fast, with a lot of fear and adrenaline mixed in, but I care about you, Summer. Truly, deeply," he said. "I wouldn't try to sleep with you just for the sake of sex, especially if you weren't interested." He spoke the last part like it pained him.

She'd craved genuine emotion, a real connection with someone for a long, long time. One guy she had dated had told her he loved her after three weeks. Something about the words or the man didn't feel right. Struck her as hollow. It didn't take too long before she realized, with an excruciating sting to her heart, that his idea of *love* was nothing like hers. When someone really loved you, they didn't let you down. Much less have sex with other people because she wasn't ready to sleep with him.

This wasn't the same thing in any way.

Logan was different. A man of his word who didn't say hollow things with some hidden agenda. So far, she believed everything he said, even the part about him caring for her. Their situation was different, too. He'd proven she could trust him with her life. Why not her heart? Her body?

But Summer was a relationship type of woman with a capital R. Okay, if she was being brutally honest, the whole word was in all caps.

Where could this go?

His eyes darkened with affection and hurt, but she looked away, emotion squeezing her chest so tight she was finding it hard to breathe.

She cleared her throat. "I'm sorry." For starting something that she wasn't able to finish. *Flirt. Tease.* Her eyes became all teary, blurring her vision. "But I can't."

"Can't what?" he asked.

For years, she'd thought perhaps she was missing the whole libido thing since most of the kisses she had experienced to that point had been enjoyable, certainly, but nothing to crave. The longer she waited to have sex, the more she had built it up in her mind, one checkbox after another of a man's necessary qualifications, layers upon layers of conditions and rules, until it had become this Mount Everest. A monster of a mountain to climb. The world's tallest. One of the toughest.

A deadly peak men should steer clear of rather than try and conquer.

An unattainable objective. One she'd never achieve.

What could this ever be with Logan besides some hot fling that would end in heartache, leaving her filled with regret?

That was why she couldn't.

"If you can't tell me *what*, at least tell me *why*," he pleaded. "Why can't you?"

Because every time he touched her, stared at her with that intense look in his eyes, Summer finally started to get an inkling of what all the fuss was about. Because his kisses could fuel fantasies.

Because I could love you, Logan Powell. Maybe she was already falling. Too hard. Too fast. How could she feel so much, want so much with a man she'd known for such a short time?

She'd cared about some of the men she'd dated, but she'd never truly fallen for any of them. Never this feeling that she had for Logan. Even that moment out on the porch with him five years ago had been intimate without touching, immediate, startling in its intensity.

"Summer, did I do something wrong?" He reached for her.

Backing away, she met his gaze and emotion lodged in her throat at what she saw in those blue eyes. She yearned for him to hold her again. But it would only lead to more kissing and touching and to other things she'd regret. She looked down at the ground instead.

"You didn't do anything wrong." Tears welled in her eyes. "It's really late. We're both tired," she choked out. "We should probably call it a night. Get an early start in the morning to search the house for whatever evidence Dani might have hidden."

Spinning on her heel, she ran inside on shaky legs before tears escaped her eyes. She was caught in a trap of her own making. A prison of standards she'd built and couldn't simply bulldoze overnight. Not even for Logan.

She fled up to the guest room, closed the door and sank to the floor with her heart quivering in her chest.

Chapter Twelve

The morning was tense. Awkward.

Logan hated it.

Grinding his teeth, he had no idea how he'd messed everything up last night. One minute, he and Summer were having a moment. Lighthearted. Romantic. Passionate. Then the next minute, she'd simply shut down and withdrawn from him.

Talk about a sour end to an evening.

Summer had gotten up right after dawn, the same time as him, and was doing her best to avoid him. No eye contact. No conversation. She wasn't even interested in the breakfast he had gone to the trouble of making for her.

As he stepped out of the room he'd been bunking in, she came up the stairs with a mug of coffee in hand. Wearing jeans, hiking boots, a tank top covered by an unbuttoned cotton shirt, she was practically fully covered today.

A stark contrast from yesterday, when she'd shown a tantalizing amount of bare skin.

She passed him in the hall without saying a word.

The scent of her sultry perfume curled around him, teasing his senses. Being near her brought their kiss back in vivid detail. The way her mouth had fit his, her taste, the snug press of her curves against his body. Every cell inside him had been cheering, *Finally*.

"I'm going for a quick jog," he said to her, and she stopped and turned around. He needed to put in a few hard miles. He wasn't a fitness nut. Far from it. The fresh air, working up a sweat, getting his heart pounding, cleared his head. Running was like meditation for him. He did it for his health, physical as well as mental. The one habit he couldn't do without. "Here's the tablet so you can monitor the security cameras while I'm gone."

She took it from him, not meeting his gaze. "I'm going to get a head start on searching the house for any hidden evidence until it's time to go meet Declan at Einhorn Industries."

"Stay upstairs and set the cameras to *Away* mode. Any movement will send a notification to the tablet and my phone." He held up his cell and tucked it in his pocket. "I'll have it on me."

"Okay."

"And take this." He pulled his gun from the back of his waistband and handed her the Glock. "You know how to fire it?"

"My cousins taught me. Out on their ranch in Texas. Do you really think this is necessary?"

"Just in case. Better to have it and not need it, than need it and not have it." For that exact same reason, he had a folded knife in his pocket. Killing with a blade wasn't as easy as they made it look on television and in movies. It was hard work and more time-consuming. But slashing tendons could be done in a heartbeat. "I won't be gone long." Today, he'd limit the run to three miles. "Twenty minutes max."

She nodded and disappeared back inside one of the guest rooms.

All she wanted was to search the house to find the evidence.

This smoking gun.

He should've wanted the same thing. Focused on the reason why he came to Montana. But Summer was an intricate part of that and right now she didn't want anything to do with him.

They'd have to leave later today to meet Declan. Maybe he would try talking to her in the truck on the drive over. Not as if she could skirt away from him then.

Avoidance wasn't going to fix the problem. Not that he had a bead on what that problem was in the first place.

Turning for the front door, he strode outside onto the porch in the muggy heat. The movement felt good even though he'd only gotten in a stretch so far. He locked the door, gritting his teeth at how flimsy it was. Anyone with half-decent lockpicking skills could get in with little effort. In less than sixty seconds. Not a decent dead bolt or chain on either the front or back door. Today, he'd rectify that. In the meantime, they had the cameras in place.

He slipped the spare key in his pocket, hopped down the porch steps and headed toward the trees. The woods surrounding the house were dense. Easy enough for someone to hide out there, watch from afar with a set of binoculars. During his jog, he'd look for signs to see if anyone had been camping out. Cigarette butts. Trash. Any item that hadn't been there the day before.

Throughout the night, he'd checked the security cameras every couple of hours and hadn't spotted anyone prowling around the house.

His phone beeped. He whipped it out of his pocket and glanced at the screen.

Summer had set the security cameras to *Away* mode.

Good. She might not be too talkative with him but at least she was still listening to him.

Get moving, slacker.

He took off on the trail through the trees. His feet pounded the compact earth. Under the shaded canopy of the trees, the temperature dropped a couple of degrees. Settling into a brisk pace, he regulated his breathing.

On his first visit out to Cutthroat Creek, he'd found this five-mile trail in the woods. Every occasion he'd come here, he preferred to use it over jogging out in the open on the country roads. The good thing about this particular trail was that it looped around the Granger property, allowing him to keep an eye on the house for most of it.

Sweat beaded on his skin. His lungs, his arms, his legs, all pumped hard. Fluid. In and out, his breath flowed in a solid rhythm. One mile into the run, he'd gotten into the zone, gliding along the path, when a flash of light caught his eye.

Logan stopped and peered through the trees. A few seconds later, he spotted that same glint. Like light bouncing off something. He looked around the area. Saw nothing else unusual. He listened to the silence. To the birds. The droning buzz of cicadas. The wind rustling the leaves. He stepped off the well-worn trail into the thick copse of trees.

Another flash of light.

Keeping his gaze on a swivel around him, he headed toward it, weaving his way around the trees rather than taking a direct path. Drawing closer, he noticed an object dangling.

A mirror.

Somebody had tied string around a small pocket mirror and hung it from a tree limb.

His skin prickled. He suddenly got the uneasy sense he was being watched. A branch or twig snapped at his three o'clock. Spinning toward the sound, he crouched at the same time.

Something whizzed past him overhead, right where he'd been standing, and hit the trunk of a tree.

A dart, .50 caliber.

Like the kind used to tranquilize an animal.

His blood pressure spiked along with adrenaline. The mirror had been bait, and he'd fallen for it, allowing himself to be lured in. Suddenly, he felt like a moth caught in a spider's web.

Click.

Click.

The sound of someone reloading. Tranq guns only held one injection. They used them on his cattle ranch back home.

Logan dropped to the ground and rolled just when another ballistic syringe tipped with a hypodermic needle, loaded with some drug, struck where he'd been positioned.

He needed to move while the man reloaded.

Jumping up, he sprinted closer to his assailant. *Click.* He still didn't have him in sight. Tracking him only by sound. Staying low, Logan crept to another tree. He peeked around the base of it. Waiting. Weighing his options. Not knowing how many darts the guy had left.

Click.

Logan ducked behind the trunk. A third tranquilizer dart bit into the bark of the tree he used for cover.

Peeking out again, he spotted the guy.

A man stood a few feet away. Dressed in woodland camouflage with a dark green balaclava covering his face. He opened the back part of the air rifle, making the first c*lick*. Pulled another dart from his cargo pocket.

Bolting up from his concealed position, Logan took off

at a dead sprint straight at him as the guy shoved the dart inside the chamber of the air rifle and snapped it closed.

Click.

Logan tackled him, taking him down to the ground hard. The air rifle dropped. Scrambling to his feet, Logan kicked the tranquilizer gun away.

The man straightened up, his fist coming clear, clenched around a combat knife with a serrated edge.

Logan squared up in the narrow space between two ponderosa pines as the other guy shuffled forward. His eyes narrowed. Logan kept his gaze on the fighting knife, waiting for it to rise, but the masked man held it low at his belly.

The man spun the knife in his hand with a skilled proficiency that told Logan he needed to take care, or this guy would carve him to pieces.

A knife fight wasn't the answer. That would be a losing battle for the home team.

Instead of drawing his folding knife from his pocket, Logan charged the man, who in turn brought his knife hand up, preparing to rip Logan open.

Logan faked in, causing the guy to slash early, and then dodged the sweeping blade. Almost. The knife sliced across Logan's bicep.

Gritting his teeth, he swallowed a groan of pain, ignoring the burn in his flesh. All his focus was on taking this guy down before he could bring his hand back up for another try. Before he could hurt Summer.

Logan stepped in close to eliminate his assailant's leverage and snatched his knife arm in a bruising grip. Controlling the blade, Logan ducked under the man's arm, bringing the knife with him while wrenching his attacker's arm into a pretzel. The guy yelled in shock and pain. Logan twisted the arm up and back, then locked his other arm around the man's neck and squeezed tight.

Locked in his grip, the man clawed at Logan's arm with his one free hand. If Logan could keep the choke hold, cutting off the blood flow in the carotid arteries, he could render the guy unconscious.

But the man threw the back of his skull into Logan's face, nearly breaking his nose. A move Logan should've anticipated.

The camouflaged man rammed an elbow into Logan's gut, causing pain to snatch his breath. Then the assailant took off running through the woods.

Eyes watering, Logan blinked away at the spots dancing across his vision. He was about to take off in hot pursuit when his phone buzzed in his pocket.

Terror seized him. The security cameras at the house had detected motion. He'd set the notification to vibrate his phone rather than chime and make noise.

Was there a second guy? Another one sent to go after Summer while Logan had been lured and baited in the woods?

Without taking the time to look at his phone, he tore through the trees, snatching one of the darts along the way. He sprinted, running flat out, his legs eating up the distance back to the house.

She has a gun.

She'll be okay.

She'll be okay.

He repeated the words over and over again in his head like a mantra, while listening for the sound of gunfire.

A good one-mile time for him was six and a half minutes.

He made it back to the house, taking the porch steps two at a time and racing through the door in under five. "Summer!"

LOGAN.

The sound of him screaming her name set her heart pounding. Summer dashed from the kitchen to the foyer with the gun in her hand. "What's wrong?"

He grabbed her by the arms, his frantic gaze flying over from head to toe, his brows pulling together as he hauled in ragged breaths.

"Are you all right?" she asked.

"Me?" he said, breathless, sweat pouring from him. He nodded.

A punch of relief hit her. "What happened?"

"Notification. Triggered." More ragged breaths. His chest heaving. "Motion detected. On cameras."

"Oh, goodness." Squeezing her eyes shut, she was mortified for having worried him. "I forgot it was set to *Away*." She looked back at him. "I went downstairs to get another cup of coffee. I'm sorry."

A muscle clenched in Logan's jaw. He bent over, grasping his thighs, and breathed.

Blood ran in a stream down his left arm.

"You're bleeding." She took his uninjured arm and led him upstairs. "What happened?"

"Trap. Set for me in the woods."

"Are you okay?" She led him into the bathroom and steered him to sit on the side of the bathtub.

He held up a dart with a bushy orange tail. "Tranquilizer."

She grimaced. Someone had set a trap for him. Intended to sedate him and then do what? To him and next her?

An icy shiver ripped through her at the prospect. She ached to touch him, to hold him, grateful he was okay and had made it back to the house. Back to her. But she'd changed the dynamic between them. Had drawn a line in the sand, for better or worse, and couldn't erase it now. No matter how badly she might want to.

Turning, she pulled out the first aid kit from the cabinet. She sank to her knees in front of him and looked at the wound. "It looks deep. Are you in a lot of pain?"

Logan's face remained pale with worry and fear. "I'll be fine."

"I'm so sorry I forgot about the sensor on the cameras." She took out a bandage and gauze. "That you had to run back in a panic."

"You're unharmed and safe." His gaze held hers, and her heart tumbled over in her chest. "That's all that matters."

She lifted the gauze to clean the wound and he caught her wrist.

"I don't want to put you through the trouble of tending to me," he said.

The hurt look in his eyes was like a knife in her gut. "It's no trouble. Really."

"I need to shower first anyway." He took the gauze from her, lowered his hand and his gaze. "I can wrap it."

"It might need stitches," she said softly, not wanting to do more harm.

"As long as it stops bleeding, I won't worry about it. I don't have a problem with scars, and when Declan calls us after he's done exhuming Dani's body, I don't want to be the cause for delay or the reason he conducts the interview without us."

"Logan." She didn't know what to say. So, she was simply honest. "You're important. Your health. Your well-being. If you need stitches, then that takes priority."

His cheeks flushed but it looked like frustration. "I guess you've got to keep your bodyguard in fighting condition."

"You're more than that to me."

"Really." He scoffed. "Can we talk for five minutes? No dodging. No evading. No running off. Five minutes of cold, hard truth."

He stared down at her, and she sensed his tension. Saw the heat in his eyes. He was frustrated and angry, and it wasn't just about what happened to him in the woods.

Summer swallowed against the sudden flutter of nerves in her chest. She owed him that much. With a nod, she said, "Yes."

A LOOK OF dread and conflict filled her eyes, but he didn't care. His objective was to get answers.

Taking a breath, he decided it was best to cut straight to it. "I messed up last night. I did something wrong, something to upset you, but I need to know what it is because I don't want to walk on eggshells or make the same mistake twice."

She dropped her gaze and wrung her hands in her lap. "You didn't do anything wrong, Logan."

"We were dancing and kissing and then everything changed. Now there's some kind of problem. Distance between us that wasn't there yesterday. I'd like to know why." Because he couldn't bear it to continue.

Face still turned away from him, fingers twisting into knots, she was silent.

"Did I go too far? Overstep in some way?" He thought he'd been a perfect gentleman. Well, maybe not *perfect*. He'd been carried away by the kiss and had perhaps gotten a little handsy, but he didn't think he'd been aggressive. "Did I misread you or the moment? I got the impression that you wanted me to kiss you. To touch you. If I was mistaken and—"

"You weren't mistaken and didn't misread anything, but I was wrong for encouraging it. I shouldn't have."

"Why not? It was only a kiss, Summer." He waited for an answer that didn't come. "You said you didn't want any secrets between us and here you are keeping one from me."

She looked up at him. "It felt like more than a kiss. Made me want a whole lot more than that with you. Maybe I'm so naive that I didn't realize it meant nothing to you and wouldn't lead to anything else."

Logan would be a liar if he said he hadn't felt the same way. The entire time he was kissing her, he'd imagined what it would be like to strip off her clothes, to hold her close with nothing between them, to be buried deep inside her. Making her groan with pleasure and cry out his name.

Even now, the thought of it was getting him hot and bothered and had him adjusting the way he sat. He'd been attracted to plenty of women but wasn't into hook-up sex anymore. It always left him feeling cheap and more alone than ever. Only one woman had held a special place in his heart. Amber Reyes. Who was now Mrs. Montgomery Powell, the mother of Logan's nephew.

His feelings for Amber as anything more than a friend had been dealt with and died out a decade ago, after he'd learned she only had eyes for his brother. Not that he and Amber had ever gotten physically close. Hugs and a few shared caresses, but not a single kiss.

Even back then, he had never experienced this bolt of instant chemistry. A gravitational pull to another human being. Not until Summer Stratton walked into his life.

Something about this woman called to him, touched him on a deeper level. This was the first time in his life that he'd had this kind of connection, and he didn't want it to end.

Logan wanted to take hold of her hand to stop her from twisting it into a pretzel, but he resisted the urge. "We both wanted more last night. Because we click." Which in itself was rare. "The chemistry is right." Off the charts. "What's the problem with a kiss leading to more?"

"My best friend is gone. So is Jeff Arbuckle. Because I convinced both of them that pursuing this lawsuit was the right course of action. Instead of having my full focus on finding out what really happened to them and making the person responsible pay for it, I'm dancing under the stars and kissing you. I didn't come here to get distracted with a fling that will only fizzle out once you go back to Laramie and I go home to Seattle. That's not who I am. It's not what I want. Two people are dead. Finding their killer has to come first. Can we please agree to concentrate on what's most important and drop any ridiculous ideas of romance?"

Taken aback by the punch of cold, hard truth, he nodded, silent for a second, letting his heart catch up to his head. "Yeah. Sure. You're not interested and that's fine," he managed, but he needed to set her straight about one thing. "Despite what you might believe, Summer, you're not the reason Dani and Jeff are dead. Filing the lawsuit was the right thing to do. Grief is natural and it's important to feel it. Misplaced guilt, on the other hand, is a distraction, too. Maybe you should work on letting it go while I keep my primal impulses in check." He wasn't an animal. He could keep his hands and lips to himself. "We'll continue investigating together and I'll keep you safe. Like I promised." He swallowed the bitter taste in his mouth. "Just as friends. Nothing more."

Chapter Thirteen

Just as friends.

Nothing more.

The words still rattled in Summer's head two hours later. When she asked him to drop any ridiculous ideas of romance, he'd looked as though she'd reached out and slapped him.

In that moment, she'd almost crumbled. Almost kissed him. Almost decided to settle for a hot fling. Take what she could have with this incredible man for whatever time they had together.

But once she got back home, she'd have regrets. Big-time. She wished things were different.

That they lived in the same city, brought together by common interests that had nothing to do with death and violence and fear, and could simply date. Like normal people.

But they couldn't. They weren't.

The lack of sleep wasn't helping either. She was going on day twelve without a solid night, and her nerves were frayed. Because someone was trying to kill her. Now both of them.

The stakes were already too high, trying to find Dani and Jeff's murderer, doing their best to stay alive while her professional life was unraveling.

These were not the kind of circumstances in which to make a life-altering decision.

Yet, she couldn't stop thinking about Logan, no matter how she tried.

After Declan called, she changed her clothes into business attire suitable for the temperature. A good pair of high heels always made her feel powerful, ready to conquer the world.

During the car ride, Logan didn't force conversation, which she appreciated, but the defeated expression on his face made her chest ache and her temples throb.

She switched on the radio, filling the silence between them, and stared out the window.

It didn't take long to get to Einhorn headquarters.

Logan parked in the lot and shut off the engine.

The things he had said, the things he thought, weighed on her. "Hey, hang on a second." She turned to him. Wanted the awkwardness swelling between them like an inflating balloon to just pop and dissipate into nothing. For a moment, she considered telling him that she was interested in him, very much so, and that was the real problem, but it would only start another conversation they didn't have time to have. "We're not just friends." She patted his forearm, and his jaw hardened. "We're a team. In this together. I know you've got my back, but I've also got yours. We're partners. Okay?"

He stared at her. For a long, long time.

Felt like hours, but it was only minutes. Seconds, really. She watched him, heart drumming.

He laughed, and she felt a twinge of hurt, but tried not to let it show.

Leaning across the console, she risked taking his hand in hers. Friends could do that. Hold hands. She'd done so with Dani many times when one of them needed comfort, the physical support. "You *are* important to me." His gaze dropped to her mouth, and it was there again, that hot flare of undeniable attraction. "I wouldn't want to do this with anyone else," she said, meaning every word. "Okay?"

He sighed, sounding resigned. "Okay. Partners."

LOGAN AND SUMMER met Declan Hart out in front of Einhorn Industries at ten o'clock sharp.

"How did it go this morning?" Logan asked, shaking the agent's hand.

"Smoothly. The medical examiner is going to give me a call when they're ready to start the autopsy on Dani's body. I want to be there for it. Also, Forensics assured me that they're going to run ballistics today as soon as they can."

Summer shook Declan's hand, looking chic in a buttoned pinstripe vest that accentuated her small waist, slim matching pants and high heels that Logan guessed were for Einhorn's benefit. Her outfits were like a little visual treat for his soul.

"We appreciate it," she said. "Thank you for not dragging your feet on this."

Declan gave a modest smile. "Only doing my job."

"When we're done inside, I have something to give you. Someone tried to shoot me with a tranquilizer gun," Logan said, and Declan raised an eyebrow. "Set a trap in the woods where I jog. I have the dart for you to analyze. We had a scuffle, and he gave me this." Logan gestured to the bandage on his arm. "Unfortunately, he got away."

"Sorry to hear about the altercation and that our suspect is still on the loose," Declan said. "Are you two ready?"

They both nodded.

Declan's expression turned stark. "Before we go inside, let me be crystal clear. You will follow my lead. You will not color outside the lines. You will let me conduct the interview. When I say it's time to leave, we go. Can you work with that?"

Logan and Summer exchanged glances. "Yes," they said in unison.

"Okay. I will hold you both to it." Declan led the way inside.

The lobby of Einhorn Industries was bigger than Logan had expected. Glossy. Polished. Walls of glass. Gleaming floors of marble. Dominating the space was a long reception desk made of a log with geometric cuts, illuminated from the inside and encased in glass. The wood must've been hollowed out with the lights added inside. Otherwise the weight of it would be massive.

As Declan approached the front desk, Logan hung back beside Summer. He was thankful they hadn't been assigned an agent who was a hard-boiled stickler for the rules. This guy was seasoned, no-nonsense, but flexible. Someone Logan could work with. He was certain it helped that they were both agents for the justice department, even if they were under a different attorney general. There was a camaraderie that translated across state lines since this particular job often drew a certain type of person. Required them to take on cases that regular local law enforcement couldn't handle for one reason or another. They operated in the backyards of others, where they sometimes weren't welcomed. It forged a shared bond that extended beyond the badge.

"Hi, I'm Special Agent Hart with DCI of the Montana Justice Department," Declan said, holding up his badge for the receptionist, "and these are my associates." He gestured to them over his shoulder. "We'd like to speak with Emma Einhorn and Chip Boyd from security."

The young woman's eyes widened. "One moment, sir."

She picked up the phone, pushed a couple of buttons and whispered into the receiver. A minute later she hung up. "Someone will be with you momentarily. Can I get you anything while you wait?" she asked.

"No, thank you," Declan said. "We're fine."

Declan joined them as they waited.

A large digital screen hanging on the wall behind the desk projected idyllic images, set to cheery instrumental music, showing how Einhorn Industries made the world a better place. Sunshine and blue skies. Kids frolicking in the grass. A Nielsen farming spreader laid down fertilizer. Adults smiled as they harvested ripe crops. A family gathered around a table outdoors, eating. The screen panned out, showing pallets of stacked bags of Einhorn fertilizer and then zoomed in on the front of a bag. The montage ended with three lines in big, bold letters, each highlighted separately before fading to the next one:

EINHORN FERTILIZER RICH IN NITROGEN, PHOSOPHOROUS AND POTASSIUM

SAFE AND ORGANIC

NO WASTE GOES TO WASTE AT EINHORN

"What exactly is the fertilizer made from?" Declan asked. "And what's the basis for your lawsuit?"

"They make the fertilizers from raw sewage sludge, known as biosolids," Summer said. "Our claim is that there are high levels of polyfluoroalkyl substances, PFAS, or forever chemicals, in the fertilizer. The product is contaminating Snowberry Creek, which runs through the Granger property and a few other farmlands. Dani convinced four other farmers to join the suit. The chemicals killed their livestock, decreased property values and may have even given some of them cancer."

"Can you prove it?" Declan asked.

"Some of it. Most of the evidence that Dani collected was stolen from her house, but she had already taken liver samples from one of her stillborn calves to be tested out of state to prevent tampering, along with samples from the other plaintiffs' livestock and water from the creek."

"Did the tests find anything?" Logan asked.

"They did," she said with a nod. "PFOS, which is the most toxic PFAS. Two years ago, the US Environmental Protection Agency proposed a limit of four parts per trillion for PFOS in drinking water. The samples from the livestock as well as the water in Snowberry Creek contained more than 600,000 parts per trillion of PFOS."

Declan gave a low whistle. "That's staggering. If samples have already been tested and you can trace it back to Einhorn, what would killing Dani Granger, Jeff Arbuckle, or you for that matter, solve?"

"As it stands now, we go to trial with only this, sure Einhorn would say mea culpa. But then we have to prove that it's causing cancer and killing people. Even then, they'd face paying nominal damages."

Logan raised an eyebrow. "Nominal being relative, I'm sure."

"Yes, but I know we can do better. Much better. I don't want them keeping this quiet, forcing farmers to sign NDAs in exchange for pennies. I don't want Einhorn to get away with making superficial changes to how they use biosolids. In my experience and that of my mentor, companies like this usually know about the potential harm but do nothing because it would crush their bottom line. If we can prove that Einhorn was aware there is a dangerous level of PFOS in the fertilizer," Summer said, "and have known for quite some time, neglecting to do anything about it, then we've got them on the hook for billions in damages. Enough to bankrupt Einhorn and put an end to their fertilizer making for good."

Down the hall, a door opened and a stern-looking man strutted out. Middle-aged. Receding hairline. Sturdy build. He adjusted his bolo tie, sliding a medallion set with turquoise in the center along the leather cord up to the collar of his dress shirt. His cowboy boots clacked against the stone floor, echoing through the lobby as he headed toward them with a sense of purpose in his step.

Another guy emerged from the same room down the hall and hurried after him. Younger. Midthirties. Lean but muscular.

Both wore earpieces.

"I'm Chip Boyd," the older man said, extending his hand. "And this Alex Pope."

"Special Agent Hart with DCI." Declan shook it. "This is Special Agent Powell from DCI Wyoming, and Attorney Stratton," he said.

Logan appreciated the use of Summer's professional title in this situation.

"Thank you for giving us a few minutes of your time," Declan continued. "Will Ms. Einhorn be joining us shortly?"

"Afraid not. She had to leave on other business. What can I do for you?"

"We have a few questions regarding an ongoing investigation," Declan said.

Chip Boyd folded his hands in front of him. "Is that so? It was my understanding that the Dani Granger case was closed."

Declan flashed a wan smile. "I never said this was regarding Dani Granger."

Logan studied the former cops. They both had deadpan expressions and stood still as stone. Boyd focused on Declan while Pope was assessing everything else, namely him and Summer.

"Where were you two Wednesday night between eleven and midnight?" Declan asked.

It wasn't until then that Logan noticed Declan Hart hadn't taken any notes. Not a single one. Not yesterday, when he had questioned them about the attack or when they had passed along every pertinent detail they could think of regarding the case. Not even now.

Logan wasn't sure what to make of it. Everything indicated the DCI special agent was taking this case seriously and throwing the full might of the agency behind it. Yet, capturing details accurately was rookie 101 stuff that Declan wasn't bothering to do.

"I was at home." Boyd remained composed, but his clasped fingers tensed.

"As was I," Pope said, his expression inscrutable. "Sound asleep."

"Why do you want to know?" Boyd asked.

"Can anyone corroborate your whereabouts?" Declan ignored the man's question.

Boyd's gaze narrowed slightly. "My wife."

"And you, Mr. Pope?" Declan's gaze swung to the younger man.

"No," Pope said with a shake of his head. "I was home alone."

Boyd lifted his hand to his earpiece like he was listening to something. Then he leaned over and whispered to Pope. "You'll have to excuse Alex. He needs to attend to an urgent matter." Boyd gave him a hand signal to leave, and the guy strode off down the hall.

"Is there a fertilizer crisis?" Logan asked, not able to help himself, and Declan slid a warning glance his way.

Boyd simply smiled at Logan and turned to Declan. "If you want this interview to continue, I suggest you tell me why you're asking about our whereabouts."

This was the problem with questioning cops or former ones. They knew how the game was played, understood the rules better than the average civilian and could stop playing whenever they decided.

"I was attacked last night," Summer said. "Someone shot me."

Declan flattened his mouth into a grim line.

"You look pretty good for someone who took a bullet," Boyd said, raking his gaze over her. "Appears as though you only got a scratch." He indicated the bandage on her arm. "But I think you had it coming."

Logan bristled. He had had his fill of menacing looks and anything that sounded remotely close to a threat. He was prepared to draw a line under it, but he also wanted to keep his word that he wouldn't jeopardize the case or make Declan reconsider their active involvement in the investigation.

"And why did Ms. Stratton have it coming?" Declan asked.

"Oh, I'd say that'd be the general consensus around town." Directing his gaze away from Declan back to Summer, Chip Boyd grinned again, and Logan's spine stiffened. "I know exactly who you are. Meddlesome lawyer from Seattle who decided to come to Cutthroat Creek," he said, a hint of Montanan twang showing on the last word that he pronounced as *crick.* "Only to kick a hornet's nest. After years of representing corporations just like ours, you've turned traitor, taking everything that you know about how companies such as ours operate and using it against us like some no-good, dirty informant."

Something in Logan rose up like a beast, ready to pounce, and he stepped toward Boyd, but Declan put a cautionary hand out, silently telling him to back down.

"How do you know about the cases I've worked on?" Summer asked, eyes wide with surprise.

"Do you really think you're the only one who can do research?" Boyd sneered. "Dig around and find something that stinks. You should be ashamed of yourself for getting Dani Granger riled up. Putting fanciful ideas in her head. Dangerous ideas that apparently caused her to relapse and drive into a tree. Ideas that made Jeff Arbuckle take a terrible tumble into the lake. You're the reason they're both dead."

Summer reeled back, her jaw dropping, as though the words had slammed into her like a physical blow. The pain in her face cut Logan to the bone.

"That's enough," Logan said, pointing at Boyd as he stepped in front of Summer to shield her from any more vitriol.

"Yes, it is." Declan cast both him and Summer a sidelong glance for an uneasy moment. Then he turned back to Boyd. "Would you please roll up your right shirtsleeve and show us your wrist?"

"What for?" Boyd asked with a look of contempt.

"Humor us and we'll be on our way." Declan motioned to his arm. "It'll take less than thirty seconds."

"Fine." Boyd unbuttoned his cuff, rolled up his shirtsleeve, held out his right arm for them to see. He then flipped his arm over, showing them the other side as well. "Satisfied?"

"Thank you for your time, Mr. Boyd. You and the rest of the security team should stay close to town for the time being. Don't leave the county without letting us know. We'll be in touch." Declan gestured for them to leave.

Logan put a hand in the middle of Summer's back, ushering her through the lobby. Once they got out of the building, he realized the physical contact he shouldn't have initiated and dropped his hand.

At the edge of the parking lot, Declan stopped them. "You violated your end of the agreement." While his voice wasn't hard, it was direct.

"I apologize," Logan said. "For losing my temper." Working a case, he was always tactical. Never emotional. But this blurred the line between professional and personal.

"That *man*—" narrowing her eyes, Summer took a breath and pointed back at the building "—provoked us."

Logan put a hand on Summer's shoulder, urging her to calm down with a gentle look. Giving him a nod of understanding, she took another breath, this one deeper, and held it along with her tongue.

He turned to Declan. "It won't happen again."

"You're right. It won't. A second chance is just another opportunity for someone to repeat the same mistake. I don't believe in them and I don't offer them. I'll speak with Mr. Nielsen and his son without the two of you."

Things hadn't gone as planned, but not so far astray that Special Agent Hart needed to hijack the case. "I have a concern with that," Logan said, not wanting to raise the issue, but it had now become necessary.

"Which is?" Declan asked, his patience beginning to wear thin in his tone.

"You don't bother to take any notes and you don't even use a recorder. After the interview with the Nielsens you might forget to pass along essential information." Other agents could handle their cases, interviews, note taking or lack thereof, as they saw fit. None of his business. Unless it involved him, and this time he had a personal stake in the matter. "We need to be there to hear the answers firsthand."

"No need to worry in that regard," Declan said easily, as if there was no need to elaborate.

"And why is that?" Summer asked before Logan had the chance.

"I don't need to take notes because I don't forget. Ever."

Logan scoffed. "The devil is in the details. Everyone forgets something at some point."

"Not. Me." Eyes hard as stone, Declan was deadly serious.

"Do you have a photographic memory or something?" Logan countered.

"No," Summer said, shaking her head. "That's the ability to recall something exactly as seen or read." She turned to Declan. "You have hyperthymesia?"

"Hyper-what?" Logan asked, feeling more clueless than he preferred.

"It's a super memory." Awe laced Summer's voice. "When a person is able to remember nearly every event in their life with great precision."

"They don't call it that anymore." Declan's tone was matter-of-fact. "It's simply HSAM now."

Logan glanced at Summer.

"Highly superior autobiographical memory," she said, explaining the acronym.

"Oh, yeah." Logan nodded like he'd heard of it.

At the sound of a chime, Declan pulled his phone out. "One of the medical examiners is ready to start the autopsy on Ms. Granger's body. They're waiting since they know I want to be there for that. I'll let you know what it turns up in addition to what I eventually learn from the Nielsens. In accurate detail. As for Chip Boyd, he wasn't the guy who attacked you, but he was lying."

"About what?" Summer asked, brushing hair back behind her ear, now looking like she'd fully regained her composure.

"Emma Einhorn didn't leave early. She's in the building."

Logan wasn't sure if he was buying the whole HSAM thing. Even if he did, that didn't translate to the other agent knowing Emma Einhorn's whereabouts. "How do you know?"

"Her car in the lot." Declan hiked his thumb over his shoulder. "Pearl gray Hummer parked in front of the sign labeled Chief Security Officer."

Logan had been far too focused on Summer when they arrived and had neglected to even notice the basics. Setting aside his emotions and concentrating on his surrounding environment was usually one of his sharper skills.

"She's avoiding us for some reason," Declan said. "Probably the same one that made Boyd get rid of Alex Pope. It rubs me the wrong way how they don't even care it's obvious they're hiding something."

Logan really wanted to call BS on Declan's memory thing. Or at least test it. "What's her license plate number?" No guarantee that he had seen it, but if Declan had noticed that much already, then, as a cop, he had looked at the plate.

Declan rattled off the license plate number like one did their birthday.

"When you questioned us yesterday, you asked us both

for our home addresses." Logan held his unwavering, stony gaze. "Mind repeating them?"

The Montana DCI special agent spouted those out too with a bored expression.

"What was the name of the nurse in the ER who spoke to us?" Logan pressed, and Summer put a hand on his forearm, now giving him a look of her own. Message received. He'd back off.

"Kimimela Anne Wheeler." Declan sighed. "If the autopsy turns up anything suspicious, then we'll have reason to haul the entire Einhorn security team in for questioning, including Ms. Einhorn."

"Please keep us posted," Summer said.

"I will," Declan said. "Let's go to your vehicle, so you can pass along the tranquilizer dart." They started walking through the parking lot. "Did you know that Snowberry Creek feeds into the Bigfork River?"

"Yeah." Summer let out an unsteady breath. "We found out from the nurse, Kimi."

"The reservation uses it for their drinking water," Declan said.

Logan nodded. "The nurse was concerned that it could be making people on the reservation sick."

"You need them," Declan said. "You need as many plaintiffs as possible. A team of lawyers helping."

"I've considered it, given it serious thought." Summer's brows drew together. "I just don't want to endanger anyone else. Two people are already dead." She raked a hand through her curls. "And an attempt was made on my life. I'm reluctant to drag more innocent people into this mess."

"You have to. No other choice," Declan said, straight to the point. "They're innocent, but they're also victims who deserve justice. Ultimately, you have to make this lawsuit so big, with so many parties involved, that it's unstoppable. Unkillable. They can't silence everyone with a convenient alleged accident. Strength in numbers. It's the only way to keep you safe."

But that would take time.

Time they might not have unless they could figure out who murdered Dani and Jeff Arbuckle and was now targeting Summer.

At his truck, Logan opened his glove compartment, pulled out the resealable bag with the dart inside and handed it to Declan.

The agent took it. "Call me if you find out anything else."

"Sure." Logan nodded. "Hey, out of curiosity, do you really remember everything, no matter how long ago, even feelings?"

"Yes. Simply seeing a date can trigger a vivid memory. Down to how I felt at that moment, like no time has passed."

Logan couldn't fathom being haunted by graphic details of things he wanted to forget, of Amber Reyes and all their interactions, each conversation, every close moment, what it had been like to want her. The striking granules of a thing kept it alive, an animate snapshot inside your head and heart. The adage that time healed all wounds was true.

Memories were meant to fade for good reason.

"Sounds like a blessing and a curse." Logan pitied the guy.

A grim expression crossed Declan's face. "You have no idea."

Chapter Fourteen

Back at the house, Summer needed to keep busy. Her hands moving. Her mind active—on anything other than how she'd messed up at Einhorn Industries with Chip Boyd.

Logan gave her space. Didn't push. Didn't force the conversation. Instead, he'd suggested that they search the house for any evidence that Dani might have hidden.

But it only led to a merry-go-round of frustration that lasted for hours.

They'd turned the place inside out. There wasn't any place left to check. They had searched every cabinet and loose floorboard and paint can. Rummaged through boxes. Probed for false-bottom drawers. Explored inside the stair treads. Looked in the plumbing pipes and vents and the cavities of every household item.

Turned up nothing. Besides weapons.

Dani had them stashed all over the house, except in the one closet where Summer had hidden on the rainy night she was assaulted.

They found a shotgun, knives, baseball bat and a revolver. Dani had been armed like she was prepared for war.

After the past couple of days, it wasn't hard to understand how Dani had grown fixated on this case until it took over her life.

Until it killed her.

"There's nothing in any of the rooms upstairs, including the bathroom and attic." Summer plodded down the steps barefoot, wanting to scream her disappointment.

Logan finished putting on the dead bolt and chain door guard and turned toward her. "You're in a mood."

"I thought for certain Dani would've hidden whatever she found in the house. Are we missing it somehow?"

Once she reached the bottom of the stairs, he gazed down at her, his brow furrowed. "You were upset before we got back to the house and started looking. Ever since we left Einhorn Industries. What is it?"

He hadn't blamed her for Declan cutting them out of the investigation. Not one harsh word from him. No shouting. No condemnation. No criticism.

Which only made her feel worse about the situation.

Her stomach growled, embarrassingly loud.

"Are you hangry? Is that it?" he asked. "We should really get something to eat anyway."

"No, it's not that. I am hungry. And angry. At myself. I'm sorry I let Chip Boyd get to me," she said, clenching her hands at her sides. "I wasn't prepared." For Boyd's viciousness, for his cruelty.

Guilt thrummed through her, strong as the pulse in her veins. She couldn't help but feel responsible for what happened to Dani and Jeff Arbuckle. If she had never suggested the lawsuit, told Dani how to go about collecting evidence, enlisted Jeff's help, they might both be alive.

Logan curled his warm hands around her arms. "It's okay. He got to both of us."

How could he be so nice and understanding about this?

A partner in her firm would have unleashed verbal hell on her while doing their best impression of Satan himself.

"It's not okay," she admitted, taking responsibility. "There were consequences. Declan Hart benched us because of me."

No second chances.

What kind of heartless person didn't give someone a second chance?

A man with a highly superior autobiographical memory who couldn't forget that every time he had given someone another chance it had backfired. That's who.

"We're not benched. We're simply playing in a different field on our own," Logan said with such conviction that she stared up at him. "We're still going to investigate Dani's and Arbuckle's deaths, using the lawsuit as our cover. Trust me on this?"

She trusted him with her life. Everything else was easy. "I trust you."

But he didn't let her go and his gaze didn't waver from her. "I didn't realize your firm represented companies like Einhorn. For some reason, I assumed you had experience working for the plaintiffs of class-action lawsuits." There was no judgment in his voice.

Still, she hung her head, her cheeks burning with shame. "There's a lot we don't know about each other."

"That's true."

"Representing the defendants, big corporations, in cases like this is not something I'm proud of. I went with the firm that made the best offer after law school. They paid off the rest of my student loan." Her parents didn't have enough to cover the full cost. "The salary was nothing to balk at and there was an attorney who fought to get me on board. Marty." Her mentor. "In so many ways, it was the right choice at that time. He took me under his wing. Taught me so much. Put me on the fast track to becoming a partner. And now…" She swallowed the rest.

"And now? I'm listening." His voice was kind and patient. Gentle.

She looked up at him, at his laser-sharp focus on her, as he listened, really listened like he was soaking up every word. Something about it made her chest tighten. Made her want to let her guard down and let him see all the messy, scary parts of her. "And now I'm throwing it all away. Because I'm here pursuing this case against my mentor's advice. In spite of warnings from the partners."

"Do you regret being here? If you do, you can go back home. Go back to your job. To your life. I'll handle everything. Continue the investigation whether Declan Hart likes it or not, though I'd rather not get on his bad side again since he'll remember it." The corner of his sexy mouth ticked up in a grin. "Chance can help me find another lawyer and a different firm to take over the suit. We can figure out some kind of protection for you in Seattle until it's resolved. You don't have to do this anymore. You can leave Cutthroat Creek."

Protection for her?

What about him?

If he was going to continue poking around in places where he wasn't welcomed, it meant he'd also be a target.

Summer had started all this. She couldn't hand it off to someone else. Ask another person to pick up a deadly mantle she wasn't willing to carry.

She stared at Logan. Even if she did go back to Seattle and he worked out protection for her, he still wouldn't be safe.

The thought of leaving him behind, in danger, while she scurried off with her tail between her legs and hid was... unbearable.

Unconscionable.

Besides, she was no quitter.

He was still focused on her, waiting. *I'm listening.*

"I belong here, waging this war," she said. "Dani lost her life because of this, because she believed in the lawsuit, in making Einhorn pay, in ensuring that they admit to what they've done. She believed in me. I started this with her and I need to be the one to finish it. No matter the cost to me."

His hand trailed up, brushing her shoulder, his fingers settling on the back of her neck, and a wave of profound connection washed through her.

"And you gave me your word we'd get to the bottom of her death together," she said. "That kind of commits me to stay."

"There are a lot of ways for us to still do this together, without you being here, in the fray."

"Are you trying to get rid of me?"

His mouth curved, a sad smile tugging at his lips. He brought his other hand up and caressed her cheek.

She pressed her face against his palm. Absorbed the feel of his touch. Tender. Warm. Full of reverence. More intimate than any kiss she'd ever shared with another man.

"I don't want to get rid of you, Summer. I want to keep you safe. The thought of you getting hurt any more, any worse…" His voice trailed off and he shook his head. "I wouldn't be able to stomach it."

Running and hiding wasn't the answer. "Someone killed Dani because she was alone. Jeff was out on that lake, supposedly fishing, alone. I was attacked because I was also alone. The same with you in the woods." Someone was picking them off, one by one, weak when separated from the herd. "But I'm not anymore. Now I have you by my side. Watching over me. Do you trust anyone else to do a better job at protecting me?"

And who would watch his back?

Logan groaned. "No one else will care as much as I do."

"About the case? About doing the right thing?" She took a breath and dared to ask what she really wanted to know. "Or about me?"

"All of the above," Logan said without a second of hesitation. He held her gaze with an intensity that made her lower belly tingle.

"Then that settles it once and for all. We stay together, get through this, and keep each other safe."

"You're a brave woman." The sincerity in his voice touched something deep inside her. "Brave and beautiful."

The tingle spread to her thighs. He had such an effect on her. But if it was like this just being close to him, how would it feel if he ever really touched her?

"I'm not brave." And she certainly didn't feel beautiful. On good days, rather attractive, sure, especially when men took notice, but not much beyond that. Maybe because her mother had taught her it was far more important to focus on what was in her heart and head than what she looked like. But she loved it when Logan called her beautiful and sounded like he meant it. "I'm terrified."

"But you're staying. You're fighting. Not running when you could. That takes guts. You're remarkable. You remind me of my brother Sawyer. He was a firefighter before he became an arson investigator. It takes something extraordinary, something special to choose to run into a burning building when every instinct tells you to do otherwise. Whatever that thing *is*, you have it in spades."

Wow. He really did give the best compliments of her life. "Thank you."

She stepped closer.

Heat sparked in his eyes, and he slid his hand down, wrapping his arm around her waist. "Summer."

"Yes."

"When you look at me like that, you make me want things."

She swallowed hard. "What things?"

"Everything."

Ditto.

He lowered his head toward hers. She held her breath in anticipation. He was going to kiss her.

One kiss had stirred up this much trouble between them. What would another do? But she didn't move away. She watched his mouth draw closer, heart thudding.

His phone rang, the noise penetrating the haze, and they separated.

He fished it out of his pocket. "It's Declan."

"Would you put it on speaker?"

Nodding, he did so. "This is Logan. Summer is with me. We can both hear you."

"The substance in the dart you gave me tested positive for ketamine. Enough to put down a man your size rather quickly. Also, ballistics came back. You're not going to believe this. Turns out that the same gun was used in multiple homicides," Declan said. "In Atlanta, Georgia. Houston. New York. Las Vegas. And Los Angeles."

Summer's stomach knotted. "I don't understand. That's all over the place. What does it mean?"

Logan grimaced. "The guy is most likely a professional."

She staggered back a step. "What? A hit man?"

"That's what I was thinking," Declan said.

"The use of a contract killer changes things," Logan said.

"And not in good way." The gravity of Declan's voice carried over the phone. "Tomorrow, I'm going to haul in the entire Einhorn security team and the Nielsens for questioning. I'll do what I can to find a connection. Also, I have preliminary results back from the autopsy. There were bruises on Dani's wrists and ankles consistent with being restrained. She was tied down and struggled. The ME found minor lacerations inside her throat and a great deal of alcohol still in her stomach."

"But she wouldn't have been drinking," Summer said. Couldn't have been.

"The ME believes something was shoved down Dani's throat."

Logan's jaw clenched. "Like a funnel. Someone tied Dani up. Shoved a funnel inside her mouth and forced alcohol down her throat to make it look as if she'd been drinking."

"My thoughts exactly," Declan said. "She also has a head wound. A fracture on the side of her skull. The blow is what killed her. Blunt force trauma. She was dead before someone placed her in the truck and staged the accident. This gives me plenty to get a warrant to have Jeff Arbuckle's body exhumed and an autopsy performed on him as well."

Everything inside Summer tensed, her stomach roiling. This was the news she'd been hoping for. Proof that Dani had been murdered. But it left her unnerved and reeling. White noise roaring in her ears. "Who did that to her? This contract killer?"

"That's what I'm thinking," Declan said.

Cold dread gripped her. "The same person who murdered Jeff. The same person who's now coming after me."

Logan put a firm hand on her shoulder. "I'll keep you safe. Or die trying. I swear it."

Chapter Fifteen

The question was: Who hired the contract killer?

Who set this entire murderous plot into motion?

They weren't going to get any closer to the answer until tomorrow. After Declan interrogated the security team.

Once Logan and Summer had a chance to process all the news from Declan, Logan convinced her that they still needed to eat a little something. They had been so focused on searching the house and cleaning up afterward that they had skipped lunch, and she hadn't eaten breakfast. He didn't want her passing out from low blood sugar.

For a late dinner, they drove to The Wolverine Lodge that Summer couldn't stop raving about. He hoped it might lift her spirits a little.

The place was popular but small. The parking lot was practically full; every table was taken, and there was an hour's wait to be seated. They chocked it up to it being a Friday night.

Summer insisted they place a to-go order since she wasn't in the mood to sit in a crowded restaurant. Another time, after they caught the hit man who murdered Dani and Jeff, they could come back, grab a seat outside with a view of the water and watch the sunset as they enjoyed a relaxing dinner.

Logan stood in a corner inside the restaurant. With his back to the wall, he kept an eye on the front door, on the hostess station where their food order would be dropped off once ready, and on Summer as she paced back and forth while speaking to Karen Perkins, Jeff Arbuckle's assistant, over the din of the restaurant.

An older woman with auburn hair, the same one they'd seen yesterday at the AA meeting, came out of the kitchen, carrying two white paper bags. She made a beeline to the hostess, exchanged a few words and hustled back to the kitchen.

"Thompson," the hostess called out.

A guy seated on the bench got up, took the bag and left.

The hostess took note of the name on the second bag, glanced around and set it inside the podium in front of her.

Logan hoped that wasn't their food, but the hostess seemed to be searching for someone in particular.

"Thank you, Karen. That's perfect. We'll see you tomorrow." Summer hung up, put her phone away in her purse and came closer to him. "The poor woman is devastated. I suspected she and Jeff might have been in a relationship, the way she took care of him, reminding him to take his vitamins, or how he playfully complained about the green smoothies she made him drink."

Logan glanced around, making sure no one else stood close to them. "Did she say anything about Jeff's death?" He kept his voice low.

She nodded. "Karen said that he often fished around sunrise or sunset but never after dark. He was supposed to come over to her house that night. Jeff was her official taste-tester, and she was trying out a new recipe. Spaghetti carbonara with homemade pasta. Of course, he never showed.

She started to get worked up, crying. I didn't want to push with more questions. Not over the phone."

Summer was kind. Sensitive. Putting the feelings of others first came naturally to her.

Although she didn't have that killer edge, the show-no-mercy kind that Chance had, Logan didn't doubt that she would be tough when taking Einhorn to court.

"When we see Karen tomorrow, can we share what Declan told us?" she asked. "About Dani?"

"No. Declan is going out on a limb for us because I'm a fellow DCI agent. We can't talk about the details of an ongoing investigation with anyone else."

The door opened and a guy breezed in. Average height. Muscular build of a man dedicated to fitness. He wore a tight T-shirt, jeans, and a compression sleeve from his wrist up past his elbow on his right arm. Gazes swung in his direction and stayed locked on him. A woodland camo cap that hunters wore was pulled down low, but folks seemed to recognize him anyway. He took long, confident strides up to the hostess, who beamed at seeing him.

"RJ!" she said brightly, fluffing her hair like a peacock preening.

Logan and Summer exchanged surprised glances.

Do you think it's him? she mouthed.

He gave her one quick nod.

"Shouldn't you be out on a hot date?" the hostess asked. "It is Friday night."

"Some of us are focused on more important things, Molly."

She reached into the podium, pulled out a bag, and stepped around to face him. "Physical connection *is* important."

RJ looked over her skimpy black dress and grinned. "Can't deny that."

The auburn-haired woman emerged from the kitchen again, carrying another bag, and hustled to the podium.

The hostess held up a palm. "One sec, Hattie," Molly said, hurling the words over her shoulder.

Hattie rolled her eyes, dumped the bag on the podium and was about to leave when she spotted Logan and Summer. Her brows drew together as she stared at them.

"How about I deliver dessert after my shift ends?" the hostess asked RJ.

"Not tonight. I'm busy." RJ took the bag from her, and Molly's smile deflated. "Some other time." He turned on his heel and headed toward the door.

Molly twisted her mouth into a sour expression.

A kid in his late teens stopped RJ and asked to take a selfie with him. RJ obliged, getting into a pose.

Molly snatched the bag from the podium and glanced at the name. "Powell!"

"Are you thinking what I am?" Summer asked.

"Yes." Logan rushed over to the podium as RJ strode past them outside. "I'm Powell."

The hostess handed him the bag.

"Hey," Hattie said with a grimace. "You two were talking to Mike about Dani Granger at the church."

"It was nothing. He didn't have anything worthwhile to say." Logan hoped that would satisfy her enough to leave Mike alone and drop it. He hurried to the door.

Summer was already outside, beckoning to him.

By the time he made it through the front door, she was down the steps, approaching RJ.

"Excuse me," she said, stopping him from climbing into his truck. "Are you Roy Nielsen Jr.?"

His eyes narrowed. "Yep. What do you want?"

"Do you know who I am?" she asked.

"Everyone knows who you are." RJ called her an indecent word and tossed his bag inside the vehicle.

Picking up his pace, Logan rushed up alongside her. "I'm Logan Powell and that kind of talk won't be tolerated."

"What are you going to do? Wash my mouth out with soap? You're welcome to try."

Logan wanted to rip his tongue out and shove it down his arrogant throat. "We're both working on the lawsuit against Einhorn Industries."

RJ pursed his lips. "A baseless lawsuit that's a waste of everyone's time and energy, if you ask me."

"We didn't ask." Summer squared her shoulders. "We're also investigating the murder of Dani Granger."

Adjusting the cap on his head, RJ lowered the bill. "I don't care about dead Dani Granger any more than I care about your unjustified lawsuit. The only thing I do care about right now is that my dinner is getting cold. So, what in the hell do you want?"

What a nice guy. Real American hero who should be celebrated.

Logan pulled out his badge and flashed it. Quickly. "I'm with DCI. Would you mind answering a few questions and we'll be out of your hair?"

RJ folded his arms across his chest. "I would mind." He looked at Summer. "You realize you're going to fall flat on your face in court and this little lawsuit will come to nothing, so now you're trying to turn an accident into a murder. Is that the best you can come up with?"

"Einhorn's fertilizer made from biosolids is toxic," Summer said. "We have the evidence to prove it. Gathering more and strengthening our case every day. Someone killed Dani Granger and Jeff Arbuckle to stop the lawsuit. But they failed. Because I will not rest until Einhorn pays for poisoning Snowberry Creek, Bigfork River and countless people."

"We'll see about that." RJ grinned. "Time will tell."

She took a single step closer to the man, the look in her eyes chilling. "Dani and Jeff's murderer will be brought to justice. No amount of money or power or influence will prevent it."

"Now, that's where you're wrong, again," RJ said. "Einhorn is untouchable. Us Nielsens are untouchable, too. I'd wish you good luck trying, but you'll need a miracle."

Logan moved in between them. "No one is above the law. No matter what your last name is. Might take a little longer, but in the end, the bigger you are only means the harder you'll fall."

RJ spit on the ground near their feet. "If you have any more questions, you can ask them with my lawyer present." He hopped in his truck and sped out of the lot.

Once his vehicle was out of sight, Summer's shoulders relaxed as she let out a long, audible breath.

"Was that the alter ego you use in the courtroom?" Logan asked, working a casualness he didn't feel into the words.

"Yeah," she said with a little nod, trembling. "It was."

He wrapped an arm around her shoulder, the way a brother would with a sister, he told himself. But when she sagged against his chest, his body's reaction was anything but brotherly. He wondered how long they were going to continue this farce, pretending that there was nothing romantic between them. "Very convincing," he said. "You made me quake in my boots."

"Did not." She gave him a playful punch to the stomach. "I didn't faze RJ at all. Only made him angry. How upset is Declan Hart going to be when he finds out that we questioned him?"

On a scale of one to ten, Logan guessed a seven.

He shrugged. "We took advantage of a chance run-in. It's not like we went to the guy's house and interrogated him. A little unfriendly chitchat in a parking lot, that's all."

"When I mentioned Dani's murder, he didn't go into a rebuttal about it being an accident like half the town."

"I noticed that, too. Right along with the compression sleeve covering his right forearm. The same arm I injured on the attacker."

"You don't think it's possible that RJ is the murderer, a contract killer for hire, do you?"

Anything was possible. "Stranger things have been true. He's got the right background for it. One thing they teach those guys in Special Forces is how to kill efficiently. But I do think RJ is going to lawyer up and remain silent."

A bigger concern was that by standing up to Roy Jr. and Chip Boyd, Summer had painted an even larger target on her back. If there was ever any doubt that she was a threat, to Einhorn interests and the murderer on the loose, after today, that uncertainty had been erased.

All this didn't lie solely on her shoulders. He shared in the responsibility. They had agreed to do this together when the best way to protect her was to keep her out of the spotlight. Hidden. Silent.

Something she wouldn't have stood for, and he couldn't have forced her to do.

He could only hope she was right, that having him at her side would be enough of a deterrent to keep anyone from trying to take her life again.

Chapter Sixteen

The sun rose far too soon Saturday after another night spent tossing and turning. After hurrying through a shower, Summer threw on jeans and a tank top, then grabbed her purse and met Logan downstairs.

"How did you sleep?" he asked.

She shrugged. "More or less the same since I've gotten to Cutthroat Creek." Restless. Her mind churning. About the lawsuit. Dani and Jeff's murders. The professional hit man. The tranquilizer dart.

Logan.

When she closed her eyes at night, her thoughts started and ended with him. She even dreamt about him. Being in his arms. At ease yet aching for more all at the same time.

"I heard you moving around a lot," he said.

"Which means you didn't get much sleep either."

"Comes with bodyguard territory." Logan grinned, and she had to fight very hard not to grin back.

"You need rest, too. We could both use a solid eight hours."

"Maybe that'll happen once we're done here and go back home."

She only wished home was in the same city for them. "We should leave. I don't want to be late and keep Karen Perkins waiting." It was kind of Karen to offer to meet them at Jeff's office after she was done making funeral arrangements. If it took her longer than expected, Summer would prefer that they be the ones to wait.

They left the house and climbed into his truck.

"I might need to be at Jeff's office for most of the day to go through everything he had on the lawsuit. Is that all right?"

"We'll stay as long as necessary." He sped off down the long drive and stopped, waiting for a tractor lumbering down the road to pass.

Summer glanced out the window. Dani's mailbox was jam-packed. The little black door could barely shut and looked ready to pop open. Summer hadn't checked it once since she'd arrived.

"Give me a second to get the mail," she said.

Logan nodded, and she hopped out.

Things were still flowing, quite literally, in Dani's life, though she was cold in the ground. They were getting closer to the truth. Summer wouldn't rest until she got justice for her friend. And Jeff Arbuckle.

She opened the mailbox. Grabbed the thick pile of envelopes. Cradling the mail in her arm, she slid back into the truck.

As Logan hit the road, heading into town, she sifted through the stack. Plenty of bills. Most stamped Past Due in red. Others looked to be letters from collection agencies.

One envelope stood out. From the United States Postal Service. She opened it and scanned the contents of the letter.

"What is it?" he asked, glancing over at her.

"A renewal notice for a post office box. Number 135." She couldn't hide the confusion in her voice.

"Any idea why she would need one?"

"None that I can think of. Dani never mentioned having it. I don't know why she would bother with the extra expense when things were already so tight for her financially." She looked back at the letter. "Dani was renting it three months at time. This is the third renewal."

"The thing about post office boxes is that you can leave mail sitting there for as long as you like. If you keep the box paid for. Otherwise, the post office will eventually return it to the sender."

"So, what?" she asked, not following his train of thought when they'd been in so in tune before.

"Makes it a good hiding spot with easy access that doesn't draw any attention. No one thinks twice about someone going into a post office. After all the trouble she had with people breaking in and stealing stuff to sabotage the case, she probably wanted a more secure hiding spot. Maybe Dani mailed herself the evidence for safekeeping."

Counting back nine months, it made sense. "She started renting the PO box after the samples and files were stolen from her house."

Summer grabbed Dani's set of keys from her purse. Looking over several on the metal ring, she stopped and held up a small brass one that was engraved U.S.P.S. DO NOT DUPLICATE. "We've got the key and with the notice we know which box to check."

He glanced at his watch. "We have a little time before we need to meet Ms. Perkins. Let's stop there on the way."

The detour was worth the time. She nodded.

At the traffic light, Logan made a U-turn going in the opposite direction from Jeff's office but headed toward the part of town where the post office was located. Within ten minutes, he pulled into the lot and parked.

"Come on." He shut off the engine.

They got out of the truck, hustled inside the post office and scanned the boxes.

"There." He pointed to a medium-sized one.

Number 135.

She inserted the key in the lock and opened it. Two manila envelopes were inside. Nothing else. She took them out and showed them to him.

The return address on both was Dani's house.

"You were right," she said, her pulse picking up. "Dani did send these to herself." She closed the box door, locking it and tucked the envelopes under her arm.

THEY HURRIED BACK to the truck, and he started the engine. "See what's inside the packages while I drive."

She tore open the first envelope, pulled out some pages and began reading through them.

With dark circles under her eyes, Summer looked as exhausted as he felt. Logan had only been here investigating for a few days while she had been doing this on her own for two weeks. Hard to imagine how dog-tired she must really be.

He pulled out of the lot and raced toward Jeff Arbuckle's office, without going over the speed limit. Surely, Karen Perkins was waiting for them by now and they didn't need the additional delay of getting a traffic ticket.

His gaze flicked to the rearview mirror to see if they were being followed. After his deadly encounter in the woods and learning that a contract killer was targeting them, there was no such thing as being too careful.

Summer was silent, reading the pages one by one, her attention completely dialed in.

"What did you find?" he finally asked.

"Precisely what Dani was talking about." A cautious

smile spread across her face but there was worry in her eyes. "The smoking gun. There are printed emails between Einhorn leadership. The CEO, his daughter, Chip Boyd and others. They knew about the PFOS in the fertilizer. They've known for over five years and deliberately tried to bury it."

"But how did Dani get those emails? Mike Johnson told us that she didn't find anything on Boyd's computer."

Summer's smile faded. She glanced at the front of the envelope. "It's dated ten days before she died."

The smoking gun that got his cousin killed.

"But Mike said that she broke into Chip Boyd's house several months back." Summer spoke while staring at the front of the envelope. "If she had found something on his computer, wouldn't she have mailed it to herself sooner rather than risk hanging on to it?"

That was a good point, especially if Dani had grown paranoid and was taking extra precautions. "What about the other envelope?"

She opened the second manila packet, peeked in it and made a face. Then she dropped something into her lap. An old, beat-up cell phone with a red case.

"This looks just like the one she used way back in college," Summer said. "Of course, it's dead."

He lifted the three-in-one multi-charging cable he had attached to the car lighter USB adapter. "One of those should fit."

The cable for the type-C port worked and the phone started charging.

She reached into the envelope, pulled out more pages and flipped through them. "News articles." She scanned the stories. "They're all about the same thing. The death of a man named Nikolai Azarov. He was a member of a Russian crime syndicate in Atlanta, Georgia. The articles are dated more than twenty years ago. And guess what else is in here?" She held something up for him to see.

Pulling his attention from the road for a second, he glanced over at it. "A bearer bond?"

"Two," she said. "Worth *one hundred thousand dollars*. Each."

Shock washed over him at the amount. "They're probably worth a heck of a lot more than that. The US government stopped issuing them back in the 1980s because they're far too easy to use for illegal activity like money laundering, tax evasion and drug trafficking since they're not registered. The main appeal was the anonymity they provided, but the treasury department will still honor them. They collect something like five or six percent interest a year."

"Why would Dani sit on this kind of money?" Summer stared down at the bearer bonds. "Do nothing with it when she was going bankrupt and couldn't afford to pay her bills? Why wouldn't she say anything to me about it?" Hurt laced her voice.

"More importantly, where on earth did she get them? What's the date on the envelope?"

Summer gasped. "She mailed it to herself *six* months ago. For six months, she was hiding this and lying to me about whatever she was doing. Oh, Dani, why wouldn't you tell me?" Summer picked up the red cell phone that was charging. "It's at eight percent." She turned it on and waited while he kept driving to Arbuckle's office.

"Do you know her passcode?" he asked.

"If it's the same phone she had in college and she didn't change it." Summer entered a four-digit number. "It worked," she said, sounding surprised. "I'm actually in."

"Maybe that's why she used that phone, for whatever

purpose, so you would be able to access it." In the event something happened to Dani.

Almost as if she knew that whatever she was doing might get her killed.

"But what am I looking for? Phone numbers? Voice-mails?"

"Maybe pictures," he said, thinking aloud. "Those are the three things most people use their phones for."

She tapped the camera icon and then the symbol for the photo gallery and scrolled. "Oh my God."

"What is it?"

"Pull over," she insisted, gesturing to the side of the road. "Now. Hurry up."

He did as she demanded, stopping on the shoulder. After putting the gear in Park, he hit the button turning on his hazard lights. *Guess Karen Perkins will have to wait.* "What did you find?"

"You have to see this. Easier than explaining it." She showed him the screen.

Pictures of tattoos. On a man's back and chest. Not just any tattoos. Familiar ink. "Those are tats only the Vory v Zakone wear. Russian mob. Those are thieves' stars." He indicated the eight-pointed stars on either side of the man's chest near his shoulders. "When worn only on the knees, the stars are a sign of someone who commands respect." *I will never get on my knees in front of anyone.* "But only the most respected can wear the thieves' stars on the chest. Means a high rank."

She pointed to a tattoo of a woman's face with roses around her neck. "Does that mean he was in love with someone?"

"No, it's the symbol that he was initiated into the Vory."

"How do you know so much about the Russian mafia?" she asked, meeting his gaze.

"I worked a case involving them once. Drug trafficking." One of the toughest he ever dealt with and rather early in his career with the DCI. "The media focuses a great deal on Mexican cartels and illegal immigrants, but the Vory have been entrenched here for decades. Their children and grandchildren born on US soil right into their illicit empires. They run a lot of drugs. Have pockets of power in expected as well as unexpected places. Like Los Angeles, Houston, Las Vegas, Atlanta, New York, even Colorado and Wyoming. They really are everywhere."

"So, our hit man is probably a part of this Vory or works for them."

"Based on this," he said, gesturing to the phone, "probably."

"What does the Russian mob have to do with the lawsuit?"

"Maybe they're a silent investor in Einhorn Industries with something to lose like the Nielsens. Or someone with a stake in this hired the mob to take care of the problem." Suits never wanted to get their hands dirty. "I don't know. Yet." But they were going to piece it together, one step at a time.

She looked back at the photos. "What does the skull with the teeth bared mean?"

"It's a sign of standing up against authority." There were plenty of others. A dagger. A spiderweb. A snarling tiger. Also, something written in Russian on the center of the back in bold letters. Whatever it meant was significant. But another detail in the picture caught his attention. "Looks like the guy is lying down on a bed."

Summer swiped between a few pictures. "But the sheets

are different in the photos of him on his back from the ones with him on his stomach."

"For Dani to have taken these means she was intimate with this guy."

"Or it means someone sent them to her," Summer said, her tone defensive. "There's more than one way for a person to get photos that are on their phone." She opened a text message.

"What are you doing?"

"Sending copies of the pictures to myself as a backup." She hit Send and moments later her phone chimed. "See, now I have photos of a half-naked man on my phone, too, and I didn't have to sleep with him to get them." Then she snapped pics of the bearer bonds.

Logan reached out to put his hand on top of hers, but caught himself, dropping his arm on the console between them. "I don't like the idea of her bedding this type of person either, but we have to consider every possibility."

The most disturbing was that Dani had gotten herself mixed up with the Russian mob.

Chapter Seventeen

Entering Jeff Arbuckle's small office, located in a shopping center sandwiched between a Mexican restaurant and a coffee shop, Summer went up to Karen.

"Sorry we're late," she said, giving the older woman a hug.

Despite Karen being in her late sixties, she always had youthful energy. An eagerness and spring in her step that Summer had envied. Now, even though she appeared a bit haggard, there was an undimmable light in her sad eyes.

"I'm the one who should apologize," Karen said, leading them over to Jeff's desk. "I should've been the one to call you and tell you about his death. It's just that it was such a shock." She pressed a hand to her chest. "I still can't believe that Jeff is gone. That I'll never see him again." Tears sprang up in her eyes. "Talk to him. Make him a smoothie. Fight with him to take his medication and vitamins."

Summer guided Karen to sit in one of the chairs opposite the desk. "The shock and your grief are understandable." She sat beside her. "We're sorry for your loss. How long were you and Jeff together?"

"Eight years. We met after I left my husband. Jeff was the one who helped me with my divorce. I didn't have the happiest marriage. Swore I'd never hitch myself to anyone again. Jeff was okay with that and my need for space a few nights a week. It wasn't the hot kind of passion of my younger days, but we found something special, something true, that we made work for us. Took care of each other. Loved each other. Deeply."

Summer glanced at Logan and found him staring back at her. But looking into his eyes, she struggled to find her center of gravity, lost in the depth of blue that was the same shade of the ocean on a sunny day. There was no denying or escaping the affection in his expression that made something in her chest shift and squeeze.

And ache.

Just as friends. Nothing more. She repeated the words in her head, reminding herself to stay focused.

Turning to Karen, Summer put a hand on her shoulder. "Did you talk to the sheriff about the circumstances surrounding Jeff's death?"

"Of course, I did." Karen nodded vehemently. "First, Dani Granger has a drinking and driving accident and then my Jeff drowns," she said, choking up. She grabbed a tissue from the box sitting on the desk and dabbed her eyes. "But Sheriff Tofteland insisted that Jeff had been drinking too much while out on the boat, must've fallen into the water, and wasn't wearing a life vest."

"Did they run a tox screen?" Logan asked.

Karen shook her head. "No. The sheriff told me that an empty six-pack of beer was found on the boat and that there were no signs of foul play."

Logan sat on the edge of the desk in front of Summer but stayed focused on Karen. "Was he a beer drinker?"

"Sure, he liked to relax with a beer at night. But Jeff wasn't a heavy drinker. My ex-husband was and I was sensitive to it. Jeff had a max of two and I've never known him to drink on the boat while fishing."

"Did the sheriff tell you what brand they found?" Logan asked.

"No, but I had the presence of mind to ask. I wanted to point out anything suspicious, but it was the IPA Jeff drank. Outlaw Brewing. He won't touch anything else. Always has some in his fridge." She sniffled and blew her nose. "I insisted on an autopsy anyway. The timing alone of Jeff's death, so close to Dani's, demanded it in my opinion. But the sheriff told me that I wasn't *family*, that I wasn't in the position to make any such demands, and there were no grounds to spend the taxpayer's money on an autopsy. Lester had the audacity to say that to me. That Jeff's death happening less than two weeks from Dani's was an unfortunate coincidence. Nothing more. Looked me in the eye and warned me to *leave it alone*. For my own good." Karen swore under her breath.

They had both lost people they loved to this fight.

Summer shared in the woman's outrage. "Shortly before Dani's death, she found what she called a *smoking gun* to use against Einhorn Industries. Do you happen to know anything about that?" They had agreed to find out how much Karen knew before sharing what they had discovered in the envelopes.

"I know plenty. I remember that day well. It was the first time in a long time that Dani came in so happy. Over the moon. You would've thought she won the lottery or something. That girl was pleased as punch with herself. But she was also worried about telling you." Karen said, gesturing to Summer.

"Why was she worried about me?"

"I can't say for certain, but I think Dani wanted to make

sure she was right. That the evidence was solid before letting you know about it. Putting together the little things,
she said." Karen sighed. "Dani seemed concerned that you
were under a lot of stress. Working yourself to the bone to
help her with the lawsuit, and she didn't want to get your
hopes too high. Didn't want you to worry."

Guilt pressed in on Summer for all the mistakes she'd
made. Chiefly, making Dani feel like she couldn't tell her
the truth and needed to hide things from her. "Dani was
risking her life with…unsavory people, doing unsavory
things but didn't want me to worry. Told Jeff but cut me
out of the loop."

"Summer, you two were best friends," Logan said as he
moved closer. Crouching down in front of her, he reached
for her hand, stopped himself and gripped the arm of the
chair instead. "More than that. Like sisters. When you love
someone, you want to protect them. Not add to their stress.
Part of loving someone is not wanting them to worry. Not
wanting them to hurt. She wasn't trying to leave you out.
She was trying to spare you."

"Maybe she did you a favor by not telling you," Karen
said.

"How so?"

"You're still alive, honey."

Logan gripped her arm, like he couldn't help, and nodded in agreement.

"You're right," Summer said. "She didn't tell me to protect me." *To spare me.*

"Did Jeff agree that the evidence was solid?" Logan
asked Karen.

"He had some issues with it, if I recall correctly. Questions about how she obtained the emails and such. Jeff
needed to depose the person who gave her the thumb drive."

Summer and Logan shared a glance.

"What thumb drive?" she asked.

"It's locked away." Karen pointed across the room to one of the five-drawer filing cabinets lined against the wall. "But I downloaded copies of everything for Jeff." She got up and sat in front of Jeff's computer and logged in.

Summer and Logan moved around the desk behind Karen and watched as she brought up the folder marked *Einhorn Class Action*. Inside, she opened another folder.

There were twenty files listed, each labeled as a date with NT at the end.

"Did you name these files?" Summer asked.

"No, that's how they came on the thumb drive. I downloaded them as is. Jeff and Dani reviewed them together, and she asked him to print out copies of the ones she dubbed the smoking gun. She took those with her."

Summer leaned in, taking a closer look. "Who was Jeff going to depose?"

Karen brought up a spreadsheet simply marked Evidence.

Summer scanned through it. Chip Boyd's computer was listed, and Dani was noted as the source. Below it was the thumb drive along with the date and name of the source:

NovaTech Data Center, Mike Johnson

"What a minute." Pressure welled in her chest. "Do you see this?" she asked Logan, pointing to the name.

"Yeah, I see it." He glanced down at Karen. "Does Mike Johnson work for the data center?"

"Work for it?" Karen said, raising both eyebrows. "No. He owns NovaTech. The company pretty much runs itself at this point. He doesn't need to be hands-on. It's the reason he has all that free time to run the AA meetings."

Logan turned to Summer. "We need to talk to Mike again."

That was precisely what she was thinking.

IT WAS AFTER seven o'clock when Logan and Summer arrived at IPS. The guys helped him unload all the files Summer had deemed pertinent and brought from Arbuckle's office.

Tak had been the only one missing but finally walked through door.

"Where have you been all day?" Chance asked.

"At the reservation, taking initiative," Tak said. "People have been getting sick. Weird stuff. They're willing to discuss the possibility of joining the lawsuit, but I think they'll need to be convinced. By a lawyer."

Chance looked at Summer. "I can be quite convincing. I'm happy to go there tomorrow, knock on some doors and round up more plaintiffs unless you'd prefer to do it yourself."

"We've learned some questionable things about what Dani may have been involved in. I think my focus needs to be on that. Figuring out what really happened to her. Besides, I believe in your power of persuasion," she told Chance.

"There was something else," Tak said. "The local water district sent everyone on the reservation a cagey and curiously worded letter." He handed it to Summer.

Logan moved in beside her and read the letter along with her. "The water district already knows there's PFAS in the water?"

Summer sighed. "This is a game to Einhorn. This letter

is a strategic move. They must have spoken with the water district after I filed the motion for discovery. Admitted that there's PFAS in Snowberry Creek and Bigfork River because they know we have evidence proving it. I had to turn over the results of the samples that were tested on our end during discovery."

"But the letter only states that there's 'low concentrations' in the water," Tak said. "Makes no mention of the potential damage."

"Why would Einhorn essentially admit that the river has chemicals in it and have the water district send out this letter?" Logan asked.

"Starts the clock on statute of limitations for those on the reservation to sue," Chance said.

Summer nodded. "My firm has used the tactic." She looked back at the letter. "It's dated a little more than eleven months ago. In less than thirty days, Einhorn won't have to worry about the unsuspecting men, women and children living on the reservation becoming plaintiffs. With Dani and Jeff dead, and they hope me out of the way as well, they can easily offer the four other families already attached to my suit a small settlement and be done with this problem."

"We're not going to let that happen," Logan said.

"No. We're not," Chance added.

Summer appreciated the support. She glanced at her watch. "We need to go meet Mike soon."

"Why didn't you have him come here?" Bo asked.

"I don't want anyone else to know that IPS is involved," Logan explained, "or that we're stashing everything here. We're only meeting him a couple of minutes away at a café he picked. Said they have excellent pie."

Eli smiled. "That must be Fowler's. I highly recommend

the strawberry rhubarb or huckleberry pie. Nothing like sweet and tart wild Montana huckleberries."

"I'm not in the mood for pie," Summer said.

To be honest, neither was Logan. "We better get going. Thanks for everything, guys."

They took off, went straight to Fowler's, and found Mike sitting in a cozy booth in the back, enjoying pie à la mode. There were only a couple of other diners seated closer to the door.

Logan let Summer slide into the booth first and then sat down across from Mike.

"Do you guys want anything?" Mike asked. "The huckleberry is out of this world. It was Dani's favorite."

Karen Perkins had picked up sandwiches, salads and kombucha for dinner and they'd eaten at the office. "We're fine."

As the waitress approached, Mike gestured to her that she wasn't needed. "Is meeting here okay?"

"This is fine, if you're good with it," Logan said. "We just wanted you to feel free to talk without fear of reprisals in case someone else overheard our conversation."

"They'll give us space here at Fowler's. Dani and I used to come here together after meetings a couple of times a month. Pie instead of drinks. So, what follow-up questions did you have?"

"Why didn't you tell us that you gave Dani incriminating information on Einhorn?" Logan asked.

"The walls had eyes and ears at the church when we spoke. There was no way I could've announced my involvement for everyone to hear. Do you have any idea what kind of liability that would expose me to? Einhorn is one of my clients."

Logan put his forearms on the table and leaned forward.

"You could've mentioned that you own the NovaTech Data Center. An important detail considering how you were able to get the information."

"Everyone knows I own NovaTech," Mike said. "It's not a secret."

"Why would you jeopardize your business?" Summer asked. "Open yourself to a potential lawsuit and loss of clients by giving Dani illegally obtained information?"

Mike set his fork down. "Dani was desperate. Doing things that scared me. Made me afraid for her life. I figured if I helped her, gave her just enough of what she needed, then she would stop putting herself at risk."

"Weren't you worried about the ramifications of breaking the law?" Logan asked.

"Of course, I was, but she had a hacker friend. Told me she could get him to make it look like there was a data breach at NovaTech in a worst-case scenario, to keep me out of trouble. She told me that you guys would only use the information to identify the emails in some boxes. Something about how it was easier to find what you were looking for if you knew what it was. You told her that," Mike said, gesturing to Summer.

Logan didn't want this to add to Summer's guilt. "Mike, how did you afford NovaTech?"

"I was already in the industry for years. When my father died and left me some money, I invested my inheritance in Bitcoin, back in 2012. Did really well. Used some of my profits to build the first data center in the area eight years ago," he said, and Logan studied him carefully. "Took a lot of legwork in the beginning to recruit clients but the business runs itself now and I can spend time helping people. Why do you ask?"

Logan weighed how much to say. "Dani had some things in her possession that has raised a lot of questions for us."

"What kinds of things?" Mike asked.

"For starters, bearer bonds," Summer said.

"Bearer bonds?" Mike's brow furrowed. "Isn't that an Old West thing? They still make those?"

Logan shook his head. "No, they don't. They stopped before she was born, which is what makes it so perplexing."

Mike considered it a minute. "Maybe it has something to do with her boyfriend. The hacker."

"The hacker was her boyfriend?" Logan asked, and Mike nodded. "You didn't mention that before."

Hunching forward, Mike lowered his voice. "The less I say about that dude, the better."

"If she was dating someone," Summer said, "she would've told me."

"Like she told you about breaking into Chip Boyd's house and stealing his computer? Or that she had those bearer bonds you found?" Mike sounded crestfallen, like he'd been through hell the last few months with Dani.

Summer clenched her fingers under the table, probably hating how much her best friend had kept secret.

Logan wanted to cover her hand with his, pat her arm, give her some small gesture of comfort. He only dared pressing his knee to hers, and she didn't pull away. "Why didn't you tell us she had a boyfriend?" he asked, circling back to it. *A boyfriend who happens to be a hacker.*

Mike shook his head as he paled. "I didn't say anything about him and still don't want to because I'm more afraid of him than the Nielsens and the Einhorns combined."

"Why?" Summer and Logan asked in unison.

"The guy is trouble. Serious bad news. I'm talking brass knuckles, scary tattoos, steel-toed boots, has friends who can make people disappear. I think he might be in the mob or something."

"What's his name? How did Dani meet him?" Logan's questions were rapid-fire.

"She didn't really talk about him a whole lot. I think it's because she knew I didn't approve," Mike said. "His name is Kirill Luzhin. She met him in Moscow."

Summer stiffened. "Dani never left the country."

"Not Moscow, Russia," Mike said. "Moscow, Idaho. I think she met him when she took her samples to be tested out of state. She mentioned a bar and grill called the Kremlin."

Summer put a hand on Logan's forearm. "She did have the testing done in Idaho, but I didn't focus on the exact location, only the name of the lab. She thought it'd be safer to do it anywhere out of state than here in Montana."

"There's a group of Russian mobsters in Moscow. When Dani started talking about her hacker boyfriend being *connected*, I thought it best that she steered clear of him. But she kept telling me how she had things under control."

"She used to say that all the time." Lowering her head, Summer squeezed her eyes shut for a long moment. "How she had everything *under control*. The moment I started to get a bad feeling in my gut, I should've pressed her for answers."

"Don't beat yourself up," Mike said, his expression pained. "Dani wasn't in the right state of mind to listen to anyone. Believe me, I tried. She was too determined. Obsessed. Nothing and no one could have stopped her."

"And it got her killed." Summer covered her mouth with her hand. "If only I had known." She shivered, shoulders hunched, looking wracked with emotion. Tears leaked from her eyes.

Logan put his palm on her back and rubbed—a reflex he needed to curb. But she leaned against him, accepting his comfort. He lifted his arm, wrapping it around her, letting her rest her head on his shoulder. He searched for the right words as a weight sank through him. A dark heaviness that drained him. Because he didn't know how to make this better for her. No matter what he told her, it wouldn't bring the easement of guilt she deserved and needed. "This isn't on you," he said, his voice low, his tone gentle. "Okay?"

Letting out a shaky breath, Summer grabbed a paper napkin from the metal holder on the table. She wiped her eyes and nodded. Then she seemed to realize they had crossed the newly established boundary and jerked away from him. "Do you think Kirill Luzhin had anything to do with her death?"

Mike shrugged. "If he was her boyfriend and was helping her, why would he hurt her?"

Of female victims for whom the relationships to their offenders were known, 50 percent were murdered by their husbands or boyfriends. "I can think of a few reasons." But how did it relate to the bearer bonds and the news articles about Azarov?

Dani, what were you involved in? And with whom?

"Any idea what would've led Dani to go so far as to get involved with the Russian mob in the first place?" Summer asked. "Take such a dangerous chance?"

"Besides desperation?" Another shrug from Mike. "Maybe she was digging deeper into Alex Pope."

Summer straightened. "Alex Pope from the Einhorn security team? What about him would lead her to Russian mobsters?"

Alarm widened Mike's eyes. "You don't know? I told

you they were shady. Why haven't you investigated them yet?"

An investigation was a process. Sometimes a marathon but never a sprint. "Just tell us what we're missing," Logan said.

"Alex Pope was born Alexei Popov. His family changed their names years ago. Maybe she found something that led her to that bar and grill."

Logan looked at Summer. "There's only one way to find out."

She nodded. "We need to ask Kirill Luzhin."

In the morning, they also had to fill in Declan Hart on everything they had learned.

"Don't go to Moscow," Mike said. "All I know for certain is that you don't want to mess around with the Russian mob. Not under any circumstances. Best to stay away from them. Please, listen to me. If Dani had, she might still be alive."

Chapter Eighteen

Summer lay in bed, staring up at the ceiling. Tomorrow, she was going to buy a giant whiteboard. Create a link chart showing everything that they knew so far about the case, persons of interest, along with the connections.

She created evidence boards when working on more complicated lawsuits. Looking at all the pieces visually tended to help. As a cop, Logan was probably accustomed to using them, too.

He might have ideas from a law enforcement angle about constructing one that she hadn't tried.

Rolling out of bed, she headed for the door as she considered creeping to his room next door and seeing if he was still awake.

Odds were high that he was. They could talk about everything, work through the details together.

In the middle of the night. With her in only a nightgown. And him in a pair of boxer briefs, hard chest bare, hair tousled.

Stopping with her hand on the doorknob, she reconsidered.

Bad idea. Unless she wanted to invite a different kind of trouble.

They were both struggling to keep their hands to themselves as it was. She didn't need to make it any harder.

But whenever she stared into his sky blue eyes, all she could think about was that kiss. His mouth pressed to hers. His hands on her body. His arms wrapped around her tight, holding her close. The tingles and ache for more. About what else he could make her feel.

About the here and now and how he had this way of making the word *long-term* disappear from her vocabulary, just with a look.

Think of the big picture, Summer.

Discussions about the evidence board could wait when the sun was up, and they were fully dressed. She climbed back into bed and grabbed the electronic tablet.

The alarm was set to *Away* mode. All was quiet.

She set the tablet on the pillow beside her and rolled over.

Closing her eyes, she tried to force her mind, and her libido, to settle down, so she could get a few hours of sleep.

DRIFTING BETWEEN A light sleep and drowsy wakefulness, Logan lay in bed.

His cell phone began buzzing beneath him, where he'd slid it between his back and the mattress. A bolt of adrenaline roared through him. Jackknifing upright in bed, he grabbed the phone and checked it.

Sure enough, it was a notification from the security cameras, indicating movement had been detected. He swore under his breath as he pulled up the live feed on the camera that had been activated.

It was the one he'd placed in the living room, covering the window in the kitchen and the others in the dining room.

A gloved hand reached through a perfectly round hole

in the window, likely made silently with a glass cutter, and unlatched the lock. The masked man shoved the window open, hoisted himself up on the sill and climbed inside the house wearing night vision googles.

NVGs?

Logan glanced at the clock on the dresser near the foot of the bed. It was dark.

The electricity must've been cut. Only reason the cameras were still working was because they had backup batteries.

Yanking on his jeans over his boxer briefs and stepping into his boots, Logan grabbed the shotgun on the bedside table. He snatched his holstered gun from the floor, hooked it on his waistband and crept softly across the room.

He slept with the door wide-open so he could monitor Summer's movements and hear any signs of danger.

Lifting the cell phone, he glanced back at the screen, keeping an eye on the professional killer. He was still in the kitchen, wiggling the stove out of place slowly, to mitigate any noise, but efficiently. The stove was connected to the propane tank outside.

Not good.

If he disconnected the hose from the line of propane, he could fill the kitchen with gas. Set something to ignite it. The explosion would cause the 500-gallon propane tank to blow as well, taking out most if not all of the house and them along with it.

His gut twisted as hot, prickling anger flooded him.

The only apparent positive of the situation was that the guy seemed committed to making their deaths look like accidents. Rather than stalk upstairs with a gun attached to a sound suppressor and put a bullet in their heads.

Logan stepped into the hall. Mapping out every floorboard that creaked in the house had been time-consuming, but it would pay off now. He treaded carefully in the hallway, avoiding any spots that would make a sound. Easing open the door to Summer's room, he wished he had lubricated the hinges with oil or bit of bearing grease.

A groan sounded. He stopped pushing the door, leaving it partially open. Glanced at the camera.

The guy in the kitchen held still. Listening. Waiting.

Just as Logan did.

Once the man seemed satisfied that no one was moving around upstairs, he went back to work on the stove.

Logan slipped into the bedroom. Summer was asleep on her side with her back to the door.

Shaking his head at her being in such a vulnerable position, he tiptoed toward her and knelt on the mattress. Eased closer. Reached over and put his hand on her mouth to keep her from screaming.

A FIRM HAND clamped down on Summer's mouth, snapping her spine straight and her eyes open.

Logan peered down at her. Then he pressed his lips to her ear. "The hit man is in the house," he whispered, and terror ran through her veins like ice water. "Don't talk. Do as I say. Understand?"

She blinked but nodded.

He glanced around like he was looking for something and sighed. "Here's my gun." He thrust the weapon in her hand. "I'll get you to the front door. Take Dani's truck. Mine could've been tampered with," he said, making her think of a severed brake line, a rattlesnake or black widow hidden inside the cab. "Do you have the keys?"

She looked over at her purse on the nightstand. The keys,

bearer bonds and Dani's cell phone were all inside. She met his gaze and nodded.

"Follow me closely." His voice was a whisper, his breath warm against her neck. "Step only where I do so we don't make any noise. When we get to the bottom of the stairs, run out the door and take the truck."

What about him?

She rolled over slightly, turning her face to his, bringing them nose to nose. "I won't leave you."

"Yes. You will."

Gripping his face with both hands, Summer shook her head. "Don't go after him. He'll kill you."

"I can't let him get away only to have another chance to try again."

She pressed her forehead to his, heart throbbing. "We have to go together."

"There's no time for this." Pulling away, he snatched her wrist, yanking her upright.

She lurched to her feet.

He grabbed her purse from the nightstand and shoved it toward her. "He's rigging the house to blow." His voice was a harsh whisper. "You have to get out."

Panic flared along with an icy jolt of fear. She shook her head again. How could he ask her to leave him behind?

Logan curled his hand in her hair, leaned in and dipped his head down. "Please," he said through gritted teeth. "Listen to me."

Then his mouth crushed against hers in a kiss that shocked the hell out of her.

The kiss was hard. Demanding. She raked her fingers in his hair, pressing closer to him. He was angry and afraid and desperate for her to do as he told her. She got that. But she wanted them both to be safe. Needed that even more.

He pulled his mouth from hers. Stared at her for a heart-beat. "I'm falling in love with you. I just wanted to say that in case…you know."

In case one of us doesn't make it.

In case he dies.

"Promise you'll leave," he whispered.

Her nerves fluttered at the dangerous gleam in his eyes. She didn't want him distracted, worrying about her, trying to protect her as well as himself. "I promise."

He held up the phone, checking the cameras, and she glanced at the screen.

The masked man, the assassin sent to kill them, was setting up candles on the kitchen table.

"Come on. Hurry." He led the way into the hall.

She trailed behind him closely, following where he walked, only stepping on the same spots on the floorboards that he used.

They crept to the staircase.

This would be trickier. Almost every stair tread creaked and groaned.

He skipped the first step entirely, landing on the corner of the second and then the middle of the third without making a sound. She'd watched him testing the stairs, pacing around the house over the past couple of days, but she'd thought he had some kind of obsessive-compulsive disorder and had dismissed it. The whole time he had been learning the house, memorizing the spots that made noise and where it was safe to step silently.

Logan truly was amazing.

Glancing back at her, he waited for her on the fifth step, where he was still concealed. Once they ventured beyond that point, anyone on the stairs could be seen from the kitchen. If the hit man looked up, he'd spot them.

Summer's hand trembled as she gripped the stair railing and snuck down behind him. Her entire body trembled. Her stomach churned so violently that she thought she'd be sick.

Logan glanced at the front door that was only a few feet away and turned back to her, searching her face.

Swallowing hard, she nodded that she was ready. Even though she wasn't. Still didn't know if she could leave him.

He skipped another step, angled so he faced the kitchen. The last two stairs he took sideways. With his hand outstretched, he beckoned to her as he stayed focused on the killer loose in the house.

Summer crept down, taking the same path Logan had. Faint amber light came from the kitchen, drawing her gaze. She hesitated.

Four candles were lit on the table.

The hit man raised his head, looking right at them.

"Go, Summer." Logan grabbed her wrist and shoved her toward the door. "Don't look back. Run!"

She bolted for the door. Unlocked it. Ripped the chain free from the guard. Flung the door open and flew down the porch steps. Dashed barefoot to Dani's truck. She snatched the keys from her purse, got the door open, jumped inside and started it. Throwing the gear in Reverse, she took out her cell phone instead of sparing a moment to even turn on the headlights. Slammed on the accelerator. Sped down the drive as she fumbled with her phone and called Declan.

LOGAN LOCKED AWAY his churning emotions and concentrated on the contract killer in the house. Shotgun raised, aimed at the hit man in the kitchen, Logan moved forward, drawing closer.

Head canted away from the candlelight that probably hurt his eyes with the NVGs on, the guy didn't move. At first. Then he reached for the gun holstered on his hip but looked back at the stove like he was reconsidering.

A distinctive rotten egg odor suffused the space. Propane companies added a harmless chemical called mercaptan to give it the offensive smell. Otherwise, the propane would be odorless.

Gas permeated the kitchen. If either of them fired their weapons, the propane would ignite, killing them both in the explosion.

"Get down on your knees!" Logan said. "Hands behind your head!"

"Or what?" the man asked, so low it was barely audible.

Logan kept creeping forward through the living room, almost at the threshold of the kitchen. "I'll shoot." A total bluff. He hoped the guy didn't call him on it.

Tension built along with the cold silence and the amount of propane gas filling the house. With the lit candles, they had minutes. Not even. Seconds. Pressure welled in his chest behind his sternum.

"You won't shoot," the assassin said, his voice gruff. "You're not suicidal." Then he sprang onto the counter like a ninja, crossed his arms over his face and crashed through the full window.

Swearing, Logan bolted after him, leaped up into the sink and jumped outside into the darkness, landing beside the propane tank.

"GET TO SAFETY," Declan said over the phone. "I'll call 911 on my way over to the farmhouse."

"Okay." Summer finished backing down the drive and stopped in the road, preparing to turn and race toward town.

An explosion erupted, followed almost simultaneously by a second larger one that shook the ground. Most of the

Granger house went up in a fireball, flames and debris shooting up into the dark sky.

Logan!

Her eyes burned and she swallowed the scream that rose in her throat. But even stronger was the rage that surged through her. "Oh my God."

"What is it?" Declan asked.

"The house! The house blew up. I have to check on Logan." She threw the gear in Drive and stomped down on the gas, speeding back up the driveway.

"No!" Declan warned. "Get out of there. Go to town."

But she couldn't. Wouldn't leave Logan behind.

What if he was hurt? What if he needed help? A hundred what-ifs spun in her head.

That professional hit man might kill him if the blast didn't. Pick him off while separated.

No one was watching his back. That was her job. They were a team. In this together.

"Come as fast as you can. I have to find Logan." Summer tossed the phone down and put both hands on the wheel as she raced toward the fire.

He was risking everything, and she wasn't going to let him do it alone.

THE BLAST HAD lifted Logan off his feet, propelling both him and the assassin through the air. Logan landed hard, the impact knocking the wind from his lungs and the shotgun from his hands. Fortunately, he'd gotten far enough away from the propane tank before it blew.

Dazed, he shook his head and got his bearings. He sucked in air along with smoke and coughed. Intense heat from the blaze bore down on him. His pant leg had caught fire. He slapped out the flames.

The other man was scrambling up from the ground, headed for the darkness of the woods. Where he'd have the advantage cloaked in black and wearing night vision goggles.

One thing Logan had learned in his years in law enforcement was that violence wasn't what set people apart in a fight. It was the distance that a person was prepared to go.

Logan grabbed the shotgun and tore off after him. He couldn't let him get away. Not again.

This ended. Tonight. Because Logan was prepared to go the distance. All the way until that murderer was dead.

The hit man dashed into the trees and disappeared.

Reaching the edge of the woods, Logan stopped at the tree line and listened. There was no sound of pounding footfalls to follow. No movement. No shadows shifting in the breaks of moonlight filtering through the canopy of branches of leaves.

Where in the hell was he?

Hiding. Waiting. Baiting Logan into another trap.

The hairs on the back of his neck rose. Logan was being watched. Sensed it. Felt it deep in his gut. If he darted off into those trees, into the darkness, without knowing where that contract killer was lurking, Logan was a dead man.

A vehicle barreled up the slight hill around the back of the house. A truck with no headlights on.

Dani's truck!

Behind the wheel, Summer sped toward him. She laid on the horn, beeping. Sticking her head out the open window, she said, "The trees! He's up in the trees!"

Logan whirled on his heel back toward the woods as the truck's headlights popped on. The bright white light shining like a beacon in the night.

The assailant whipped his head away from the harsh

glare, throwing his arm up to shield his face. Losing his footing on a branch, he fell, hitting the ground.

Behind him, Logan heard the truck skid to a stop and the door open, but he lifted the shotgun and pointed at the guy.

Ripping off the night vision goggles with one hand, the hit man drew his gun with the other hand.

Logan put his finger on the trigger and pulled it.

Thunk. The weapon didn't fire.

Jammed.

He'd only made certain that it was loaded and hadn't taken the time to properly test Dani's shotgun.

The other guy rose up on his knee, taking aim—dead center on Logan.

Three shots fired. *Bam! Bam! Bam!*

Logan's heart lurched as he froze. Expecting pain that didn't come. He glanced down at his chest. No blood. No wounds.

Then he realized the loud shots hadn't been fired from the sound suppressed gun. He looked back over his shoulder. Summer was standing not far behind him, Glock in her hands, still raised like she was prepared to fire again. At the sight of her, he lost another piece of his heart.

Logan spun back toward the threat in time to watch the masked man keel over onto the ground. He hurried to him and picked up the man's gun. Yanking off the black balaclava, Logan revealed an unfamiliar face. Checking for a pulse, he pressed two fingers on part of a spider's web that had been tattooed over the man's carotid artery, covering half his neck. The guy was part of Vory, connected to the Russian mob. Whoever he was, the stranger hadn't been the man in the photos on Dani's phone. The guy Logan suspected she'd been sleeping with didn't have any ink on his neck.

"He's dead!" Logan stood and headed toward Summer. Lowering the gun, she ran to him and practically jumped into his arms. His heart was lighter than air. He wrapped her in a bear hug, lifting her from her feet, never happier to see or touch anyone in his life. Holding her close, he tightened his grip on her, determined to never let her go.

Chapter Nineteen

The EMTs had given Summer and Logan foil blankets to wrap around themselves after the medics insisted on examining them. Logan's lower leg had been treated for minor burns. Summer was astounded that he had refused painkillers, but his tolerance was clearly higher than hers.

Declan finished taking their statements as Logan held her hand. "Why didn't you let me know last night about this Kirill Luzhin in Moscow, Idaho?"

"I have the same question," Chance said, who'd brought Logan some clothes since he'd lost everything in the explosion.

Summer had only packed an overnight bag's worth of stuff and most of her things were still at the cabin.

Logan sighed. "I couldn't discuss an active investigation with you," he said to Chance. He looked at Declan. "I knew you had your hands full questioning the Einhorn team and Nielsens. I don't expect you to work around the clock. Figured I would let you know first thing in the morning."

Flattening his lips in a grim line, Declan shook his head. "Well, it's morning now," he said, gesturing to the lightening sky.

It was almost 5:00 a.m. and hard to believe that it was already Sunday. But she was grateful to see the sun rise after the night they'd had.

No arrests had been made, so she assumed Declan's interrogations yesterday hadn't produced much. "How did the interviews go with Einhorn and the Nielsens?"

Declan shook his head. "They all lawyered up. Barely answered any questions."

"Were you aware that Alex Pope was born Alexei Popov?" Logan asked.

"No, I wasn't. But I did find out that the homicides our guy here—" Declan hiked his thumb at the body bag "—is most likely responsible for are all loosely or closely related to the Russian mafia. There's a link to Einhorn or Nielsens. Maybe it's through Pope. Or should I say Popov. Whatever it is, if it exists, I'll find it. Kirill Luzhin might be the key."

Chance clasped Logan's shoulder. "I understand not telling me about the autopsy results, but you should've at least told me you were dealing with a Russian mafia hit man. I could've provided more support."

Logan shook his head. "You've done so much as it is. You and the IPS team are still doing a ton, going through the discovery."

"At least we know what we're looking for now," Chance said, "which should it make the process go faster."

Dani had made sure they had what was needed. "If those emails aren't there, we'll have to file a court order to have Einhorn disclose all corporate communications."

"Why wait?" Chance asked with a shrug. "I say we file tomorrow."

"We could request the court go through a third party," Summer said. "Have NovaTech legally turn over all of Einhorn's digital documentation to ensure nothing is excluded or deleted." Thanks to Dani connecting the dots that NovaTech was the key, that the data center housed all of Einhorn's secrets, and verifying it, they would have everything they needed for an airtight case.

"Stick to the lawsuit," Declan said. "I'm ordering both of you not to question anyone else regarding the deaths of Dani Granger, Jeff Arbuckle, and the attempts made on your lives."

Logan's jaw clenched. "But I wanted to go to Moscow. Talk to this Kirill Luzhin in person."

Declan raised his palm "Leave it to me. You two have been through enough. You're lucky to be alive."

"Listen to the man," Chance said.

"Luck has nothing to do with it. I'm alive because of Summer." Logan curled an arm around her shoulder. "Without her, I'd be dead."

She'd almost lost him. That hit man had had him in his sights. Ready to kill him. If she'd left him alone, he would be dead. Gone. Leaving a hole in her life and her heart.

All this time, she had been focused on long-term, and it was still important to her, but so was recognizing when she found someone special, when what they shared was not only meaningful but also profound and making the most of whatever time she had with him.

Resting her head on Logan's chest, she wrapped both arms around his waist. She might never feel this way about anyone ever again. The real regret would be walking away from him not knowing what might've been between them. Whether it lasted for a month, a week, or mere days.

However long they could be together, not holding back, she'd cherish it for the rest of her life. Deep in her heart, that was what she really wanted. To share her heart and her body with someone who felt the same about her as she did about him. Who truly cared. Who respected her.

Whom she could trust completely.

Everything that mattered she already had with Logan.

"Your stubbornness paid off." Declan eyed her. "This time." A sheriff's office vehicle pulled up and Declan turned around. "Don't push it. Both of you need to stand down. Get some rest and keep a low profile. This isn't over yet. We still need to figure out who hired the assassin. I'll contact the sheriff of Latah County, Idaho, and arrange backup to go with me to this Kremlin bar and grill. Today. I want to get to the bottom of who's behind all this."

Summer unzipped her purse, took out Dani's old cell phone, the news articles and the bearer bonds, and handed them to Declan. Then she gave him the passcode. "See if Kirill has tattoos on his body that match the ones in the photos."

"I'll do my best. As for this—" Declan gestured to the sheriff's vehicle "—and everything else, let me deal with it." He headed to the cruiser as Lester Tofteland stepped out. "Sheriff, this is a DCI crime scene. I'll be happy to give you a copy of my report once the case is closed. For now, your presence and your involvement are neither needed nor wanted."

"I think he's got that in hand," Chance said to Logan. "Do you guys need a lift or a place to stay?"

"We've got my truck. Just need to check it out and make sure it's safe first," Logan said.

"And I still have the cabin that I'm renting."

"The one-bedroom?" Chance asked, raising an eyebrow in a way that made her squirm.

"I'll take the sofa." Logan tightened his grip on her. "Or sleep on the floor."

"Sure you will." Chance pressed his palms together and rubbed them. "I'll help you check your truck and then you two can sort out your sleeping arrangements without my interference."

AFTER SHUFFLING INSIDE the cabin and locking the door, Logan took Summer's hand and sat down on the sofa with her.

"There's been tension between us since I kissed you. We could stay with Chance if you prefer. I love the guy, but he can be a lot."

"Yes, he can. No offense to your friend."

He smiled. "I just don't want to put you in an uncomfortable position by us staying here together."

She scooted closer, pressing her leg to his. "*You* don't make me uncomfortable, Logan. My feelings for you do."

"I understand."

"Remember how I told you that kissing you made me want more? A lot more?"

"Yeah."

"That was the problem."

"But why?" He wanted more every time he touched her, heck, looked at her. In his book, that wasn't a problem, it was a gift. Something rare that should be treasured.

"I've never been with a man," she said, spitting the statement out like it was a bad thing and hanging her head as though ashamed. "I'm a virgin."

He took in her words, letting them roll around in his head for a moment. "Okay." How that was a problem still eluded him. "Are you waiting for marriage? If you are, I'm fine with that."

Her head whipped up, and she stared at him as though he'd started speaking a foreign language. "Really?"

"Sure." He nodded. "I respect you, Summer, and your values." Nothing wrong with being old-fashioned.

She huffed a breath. "I'm not waiting for marriage."

This woman had his head spinning with confusion. "I

don't understand. Then why haven't you been with anyone yet?"

"Because I want it to mean something. Not for it to be some empty physical act. I want it to be special, with someone I care about."

Sounded reasonable to him. "All right."

"Someone I'm in a relationship with. A relationship that has long-term potential. I get that not all potential is realized, but I don't want a fling. I want the person I'm going to be intimate with to want the same thing, to have the same intention. For the end goal to be a commitment. Or at least, I did, until you were nearly shot and I almost lost you."

Summer knew exactly what she wanted and shouldn't have to settle for anything less.

He admired that about her. "We care about each other. It's been fast, but I already know you're the type of woman who wants to take things slowly."

"I don't need slow. Not if it feels right. But I backed off the other night because I thought I needed long-term potential. And that's something we don't have."

"Why not?"

Her face twisted in confusion again. "Logan."

"Hear me out," he said. "After we met at the funeral for Dani's mom, I've thought about you. About the way you swept in and handled everything, so that Dani and her father didn't have to. About how you cleaned up late into the night without a single complaint."

"You did help me. Without complaint, too."

"I've thought about your smile. About your kindness. Your warmth." The smell of her, sensual and sophisticated. The sound of her laugh. "How I wanted to keep talking to you." Like they could talk forever and never run out of things to say to each other.

"But that was five years ago," she said, and he couldn't ignore the sadness in her eyes.

"Exactly." Interlacing his fingers with hers, he grinned. "I have to be honest about something else. I didn't only come here because I was needed. I came because I knew you'd be here. I didn't want to miss another chance at this."

Her eyes grew wide, and she tensed.

"Do you think less of me?" he asked.

She shook her head. "You saw a need and you filled it. You did it for Ric, you did it for Matt, and it's okay that you also did it for yourself. I think it's important for people like you, who give of themselves so easily, without asking for anything in return, to sometimes be a little selfish and take what they need."

Summer was exceptional. Singular.

"But I'm not sure what to do with all that," she said. "How does it erase the obstacle of distance when you go back home?"

Logan recognized Summer was a logical woman. One who strategized and planned. Details were important to her.

"I have a proposal," he said. "Let's explore what we feel. I want to kiss you again and hold you and not be afraid to do it. In exchange, I promise that we won't cross the line. We won't go to fourth base in the heat of the moment." Nothing wrong with second. Possibly even third. "We'll discuss it beforehand, without emotion clouding our judgment. As for a relationship, we're kind of sort of already in one. We just skipped the dinner and dancing parts."

"We are in something together. For however long we're here. Then we go our separate ways, I guess."

"A flight from where I live to Seattle is only three hours." Technically, he had to drive two hours to Denver for the flight, but he was fine with that. Not as though they were based on opposites coasts or had an ocean between them. This was doable. "Only logistics. Though if that's all too much of a headache for you, then I understand."

Somehow, he'd manage even though staying away from her would be like torture.

"It's not a headache," she said, surprising him. "It's a relief because I want more of all that with you, too." She smiled. "In my head, I was making it big and complicated. Insurmountable. But I like the way you see things. How you simplified it."

"We have to start somewhere, right?"

"According to you, we've already started. It was only a matter of how to proceed. Have you done this before, a long-distance relationship?"

"No."

"Have you ever been in love?"

"I thought I was when I was younger. With Amber Reyes, Chance's sister."

"Your sister-in-law?" Summer asked, deadpan, her eyes growing wide.

"It was years ago," So far in the past, he had been a different person. "We were just teenagers. But she only ever had eyes for my brother. Amber and I never dated. Never shared anything more than a few hugs. I had confused infatuation with something more. Truth be told, the only woman I've ever truly fallen for has been you."

She rocked back a little, still holding his hand. "Back at the house we were scared, and adrenaline was flowing. You don't have to say that now. It's not necessary."

"You're right, I don't. But it's true. I won't ever say something I don't mean. No secrets between us. No lies." He didn't want anything to get in the way of what he could have with Summer.

She slid her fingers into his hair and brought his face closer, but he was the one to kiss her. Cupping the back of her head, he licked into her mouth. The touch of her tongue sent a surge of heat pumping through him. Her arms came around his neck, and he pulled her closer, hauling her onto his lap. She tasted even better than last time. Hot and sweet. So good.

So perfect.

He'd wished he had called Dani a few months after her mother's funeral and got Summer's phone number. Even her address. Just showed up at her door and asked her out on a date.

Maybe that would've been too much, but he sensed she would've appreciated the grand gesture, especially if he had booked a hotel room for himself and made it clear he was only there to take her out, no strings attached.

The kiss deepened, growing more heated. She was clinging to him, moaning in his mouth. This thing between them felt completely right. Like every kiss before her had been a weak imitation of what it should be.

He eased back, and she blinked up at him with a dazed look.

"Wow," she said, breathless.

"Yeah." He wanted a lifetime of *wow* with her.

Chapter Twenty

A silver lining.

This thing she'd found with Logan, this relationship, was the one silver lining that had come from all the death and horror.

Summer and Logan had cleaned up and tried resting. Rest turned into making out and cuddling on the bed. They might have dozed off here and there in between kissing and touching and aching for more.

But he had made a promise and she liked ground rules. It was one of the reasons she loved practicing law.

They went out and purchased a giant whiteboard like she wanted. She already had a wireless printer and scanner. They discussed the details of everything they'd learned. Printed out pictures of the bearer bonds and the unknown tattooed man. Spent the rest of the day identifying the people of interest, mapping out all the facts, and listing their theories as to who hired the hit man. Their only consensus was that it was someone who didn't want to get their hands dirty. Who wanted distance from the murders.

"We need a break from this," Logan said. "Your stomach is starting to growl."

She hadn't even noticed, too preoccupied with the evidence board. "I guess you're right."

"Let's go to The Wolverine Lodge. Try to get a table overlooking the water and watch the sunset while we eat."

Dani's death had been proved a homicide. The hit man was dead. They had survived. Those were causes for celebration. "Give me a minute to change into something nicer."

"Why? You already look great."

She glanced down at her tank top and jeans and frowned. "This is our first official date. I want to change into something you'll remember." The comment made her think of Declan. Born with the boon and burden of remembering everything, and something about it made her sad for him. "I won't be long."

"When you say that, should I turn on the TV and prepare to wait for an hour?"

"Five minutes. Not a second longer." Not the sort to agonize over an outfit, she was always decisive and only purchased quality items that flattered her figure. Besides, it wasn't as if she had access to her entire wardrobe. She'd brought two large suitcases of clothes, not knowing exactly how long she was going to be there.

She hustled into the bedroom and opened her suitcases. One thing immediately stood out. A halter-strap fuchsia dress that hugged her torso and accentuated her cleavage, with an A-line skirt sprinkled with blue and yellow flowers along the bottom. She paired it with comfortable espadrille wedge sandals with straps that tied at the ankles and made her feel like she was walking on a cloud. Quickly, she brushed her hair, smoothing out the curls, and applied a little makeup to freshen up her face and hide the dark circles under her eyes. A spritz of the perfume Logan liked and she was ready in four minutes.

"Ta-da!" she announced, opening the door and strolling out of the bedroom.

Logan whistled. "You look so hot I would've waited an hour without complaint."

She suspected Logan would've waited without complaint regardless of what she wore. "Thank you," she said, doing a little twirl. "Mind if we walk? It's only a mile and it's a cooler day." The weather was beautiful. Mild. Sunny. Not too windy.

"Not at all. I didn't get to jog today. It'll be good to stretch my legs." He pocketed his keys, hooked his holstered gun on his waistband, put his cowboy hat on his head and they left.

They held hands as they strolled.

She loved the route to the restaurant. Once they crossed the creek, they could take the walking path adjacent to the lake. Logan could jog there while they stayed at the cabin.

At the crossing of Cutthroat Creek, they came to the quaint covered bridge that had a weeping willow on one end and a flowering purple tree on the other.

"I love this little bridge," she said. "It looks like something plucked out of a Thomas Kinkade painting."

Right before they entered, he pressed her up against the railing. His hands settling on her waist, stirring tingles in her thighs. "And you look like something plucked straight out of one my fantasies."

"Oh, really?"

Dipping his head closer to hers, he nodded. "I never say anything I don't mean."

She slid her arms around his neck and kissed him. He dug his fingers into her hair and pulled her against him. His tongue tangled with hers, his wide shoulders under her hands, his body pressed against her.

The kiss was hot and hungry and the raw fierceness of it sent a shot of desire straight to her core.

One of his hands slid lower, cupping her butt, bringing her pelvis close against him. Awareness flooded her body as she felt the hard ridge of him through his jeans. Desire pumped through her hard and she arched her back, pressing her breasts to his chest. Combing her fingers up into his hair, she rocked her hips against him. He pulled her in even tighter, as though they couldn't get close enough.

She loved the way he kissed. How he tasted. She loved the way he smelled. Touched her like something precious and irreplaceable that he didn't want to lose.

His phone rang and he groaned. Slowly, he pulled away like it hurt to let her go and gazed down at her.

She saw desire burning right along with frustration in his deep blue eyes. Sliding her hands over his muscular shoulders, she rose up, giving him one more quick kiss on the lips. "Answer it."

"I want to shut the world out. Focus only on you and me for just one day."

She caressed his cheek. "We'll get the chance. Eventually."

Logan's phone continued to ring.

Instead of answering it, he wanted to go back to kissing Summer. She was wearing a sexy dress. Smelled so good. Her face glowing, either from the walk or kissing. She looked relaxed, at peace, he dared think even happy.

"I'm a lucky man to have you in my life." That she wanted him in the same way he wanted her. He'd never been so drawn to someone, like iron to a lodestone.

"No luck involved. You're the best man I know."

His phone stopped. "If it's important, they'll leave a message," he said, and they started walking under the bridge.

Summer's phone now rang.

The hairs on the back of Logan's neck rose and he got the sense they were being watched. Putting his arm around her, he glanced over his shoulder.

There was an old truck idling down the road. License plate obscured with a thick layer of mud. With the visor down and angle of the sun, he couldn't see the driver.

Dread tightened his gut.

"It's Declan," she said. She answered, "Hi. Logan is here with me and you're on speaker."

"I'm in Moscow." Declan's voice was strained. "Everything went to hell in a handbasket."

"What do you mean?" she asked.

Logan kept his gaze on the truck. Picking up their pace, he wanted to hurry to the other side of the bridge.

"There was a shoot-out. Two deputies are dead. Two more were wounded. We questioned a few thugs that we caught. Only one talked. I showed him the pictures of the tattoos. He translated the Russian word inked on the man's back. Means Azarov. The same name from the news articles. And get this. Kirill Luzhin doesn't exist. The name is a code word for trouble. If anyone came in there looking for a man by that name meant that person should be killed on sight, no questions asked. The Kremlin was a trap."

Mike Johnson.

"If Mike Johnson was your only source on this Moscow tip," Declan said, "then it's him."

They both heard the angry rumble of the truck at the same time. Engine revving behind them, the truck shot off down the road, tires spinning, rubber burning, barreling toward them.

Now that they were under the covered bridge, with two sides walled off, they were vulnerable.

Trapped.

"Run." Logan nudged her forward. Spinning around, he drew his gun. "Get off the bridge, Summer!"

The big truck sped under the covered bridge, bearing down on them.

Logan planted his feet in a wide stance, controlled his breathing, held his hands steady and took aim at the windshield. Driver's side. He pulled the trigger, firing four bullets.

The truck swerved back and forth, like the driver struggled to maintain control, but the vehicle kept coming straight at him.

He unloaded two more shots at the tires.

Veering sharply away—mere feet from Logan's position—the truck plowed into the side of the bridge. The tail end narrowly missed sideswiping him and the front crashed through the solid wood wall, but the vehicle was in no danger of tipping over the edge.

With his weapon trained on the driver's-side window, Logan hustled to the truck. He yanked open the door with his left hand, keeping the gun raised. Ready to shoot.

A single man sat behind the wheel. Deflated air bag in his lap.

Mike Johnson was slumped to one side. Baseball cap tucked low. Sunglasses covered half his face. Gunshot wounds in his chest. Blood soaking through his shirt. His shaking hand reached for a gun on the console.

Stepping up on the running board, Logan snatched the weapon from Mike's fingers and shoved it in his waistband, pressed against his spine. After making sure the guy didn't have any other weapons close at hand, Logan holstered his gun. He unclicked the seat belt, dragged Mike out of the truck and laid him on the ground.

Kneeling beside him, Logan looked over his injuries.

Without immediate medical attention, Mike wasn't going to last long.

Summer ran back over, coming up alongside them. "I called the police. An ambulance is on the way."

"No ambulance." Mike shook his head. "Better to let me die here than the hell they'll put me through in prison."

"Who?" Logan asked.

"My family. I'm supposed to be dead already. If they find out that I'm still alive, my punishment will be worse than death."

Summer crouched near Mike's head. "You're Nikolai Azarov."

Mike, Nikolai, nodded.

"But why?" she asked. "Why did you kill Dani?"

"She knew I was in love with her. Used it against me. Slept with me. Made me think that she felt the same. Only to ask me to search Einhorn Industries records. To get her incriminating evidence."

"And you told her no," Logan said.

A man in hiding from the mafia, with everything to lose, wouldn't want to risk exposure in something like a lawsuit.

Mike nodded. "Dani wouldn't let it go, but I didn't realize that until she showed me what she'd found. What she'd pieced together about me."

"She searched your house," Summer said. "Found the bearer bonds."

"I stole them from my family. To start over. Faked my death for a clean slate."

"Dani took the pictures of your tattoos and must've had the word on your back translated." Summer's eyes welled with tears. "Dug into the name Azarov and figured out who you really were."

Swallowing hard, Mike nodded again. "She blackmailed

me into giving her the Einhorn information. Promised she'd destroy the evidence about my identity. Give back the bearer bonds. That we could be in a real relationship." He took a wheezing breath, and Logan could tell that his lungs were filling up with blood. "But then Jeff Arbuckle wanted to depose me. Dani tried to convince Jeff that the information was leaked from a data breach of NovaTech, but Jeff insisted that I had to be deposed. No way around it. I couldn't risk that, and Dani refused to get rid of the files I'd given her. Told me that everything had gone too far. That she needed them. For the lawsuit. She left me no choice. I had to make it all go away."

"There's always a choice," Logan said. "You just made the wrong one."

Sirens wailed in the distance, drawing close.

"Dani cared for you." Summer clenched her hand into a fist. "And you killed her."

"I loved her. Trusted her." Mike coughed up blood. "Let her see my body. My life in ink. Let her have free rein of my home. And she betrayed me. Because she didn't care about me. Not enough. She was going to ruin my life. The only thing that mattered to her was the lawsuit."

"I don't think she ever wanted to expose you," Summer said. "When she took those pictures of you, she tried to protect you by not showing your face. She never told me about you or the bearer bonds, or the NovaTech files. She must've thought that she could come up with a workaround with Jeff to keep you out of it."

"She failed," Mike said. "I tried to have my mess cleaned up. But you two just wouldn't die. A couple of more accidents and I would've been free. Would have been safe."

If he survived, he was going to answer for all his crimes.

Mike clutched Summer's forearm. "I'm sorry." Another wheeze. "Dani suffered." He shook his head, his face wrenched in pain. "Wanted it to be quick. Told him… the man I hired to make it…look like an accident. Quick."

A sheriff's cruiser pulled up along with an ambulance.

Mike's hand slipped from Summer's arm and fell to the pavement. His head lolled to the side. Eyes open but seeing nothing. He was dead.

Logan took her hand and stood, pulling her up beside him. He moved her away from the body and held her. "Everything is going to be okay."

It was over. The men who'd tried to kill them were gone.

Summer was safe.

A battle still had to be fought with Einhorn Industries in court, but the worst of it was behind them.

Now they could focus on the future.

A future together.

Chapter Twenty-One

Three weeks later

"Congratulations," Logan said, seated across from Summer at an outside table overlooking the lake at The Wolverine Lodge. He raised a glass of wine the waiter had poured moments ago. "Here's to making Einhorn Industries pay."

Once they got the emails, legally, from NovaTech, and showed the opposing counsel their smoking gun, Einhorn had settled out of court. For billions that would be paid out to the plaintiffs, the other farmers and the people on the reservation who had joined the lawsuit.

Smiling at him, she was unable to tamp down the elation rising in her chest. With Logan in her corner, covering her back, she felt as though she could take on the world. "Thank you. But it was a group effort. I couldn't have done it without Chance and the other guys at IPS. *And you.*"

"With Einhorn shutting down and forced to clean up Snowberry Creek and the Bigfork River, people won't have to worry anymore."

Someone approached their table.

Hattie. The woman with auburn hair who had been at the AA meeting and worked at the restaurant. She set a breadbasket down in front of them. "I read in the *Beacon* what you two did. Catching Mike Johnson and exposing the dirty truth about Einhorn's fertilizer." She pursed her lips. "I tried to warn you two about Mike."

"Warn us?" Logan asked. "When?"

"The night you came in and picked up a to-go order. I was trying to tell you that there was something fishy about the way Mike had been acting. I've known that man for twenty years since he moved here. Not once had I ever seen him pose for a photograph. The man avoided cameras like a vampire avoids sunlight, worried they'll be incinerated into ash. Know what I'm saying?" She narrowed her eyes. "Then out of the blue, at Dani's five-year sober celebration, he whips out his phone and insists someone takes pictures of the two them. They both smiled like nothing was wrong, even though I'd seen them arguing days before. Mike could be a little scary at times. Next thing I knew, Dani turned up dead, I started thinking how convenient it was that Mike had a picture of the two them as bosom buddies. Grinning. As though he wanted proof there was no ill will between them. A distraction from the truth."

Mike was good at distractions. Alex Pope's family had changed their names from Popov, but not for nefarious reasons. He'd only mentioned it to keep them looking in the wrong direction. Then there was the *hacker*, who was really him, and the setup at the Kremlin, using the fictitious Kirill Luzhin, whose name was a code word to have them killed. Mike Johnson had been full of deadly secrets.

"Did you ever mention Mike's odd behavior to the sheriff?" Logan asked.

"No. I didn't have any proof," Hattie said. "Only a hunch. But I did tell Sheriff Tofteland that Dani was five years sober and didn't seem as if she was on the verge of a bender. He dismissed me like I had a screw loose in my head. So, I went to Mike and asked him if he did the same. You know, tell the sheriff the truth. Mike told me it wasn't his business. Didn't want to get involved. Warned others in AA to stay out of Einhorn's way. That didn't sound like a bosom buddy to me."

Summer touched Hattie's arm. "Thank you for telling us now. For caring about Dani."

"I'm just glad you got justice for her. For her and Jeff Arbuckle. And all those people poisoned by Einhorn." Hattie shook her head. "An evil thing they did, fooling us into believing the fertilizer was safe. But even braver of you to take them on. I spoke to the manager and your meal is going to be comped. Enjoy dinner on us tonight. Everyone thanks you."

Emotion clogged her throat at Hattie's words. All Summer could do was nod before the woman walked away.

Logan reached across the table and took her hand. "Are you okay?"

"When I came here and people realized I was the lawyer leading the war against Einhorn, they hated me. Now..." She shrugged.

"Now they see you for who you really are. Not someone here to ruin but to rescue. Dani would be proud of you."

Summer liked to think her best friend was looking down on everything and smiling.

"Instead of folks treating you with disdain," Logan said, "you'll get the admiration you deserve."

"It will be nice to be greeted with a smile rather than a scowl since I'm going to be here indefinitely." She was already looking for a house to buy.

With the big win, her firm would get its cut and then she wanted to move on. Someone had to monitor the health of people who still might eventually get sick from the chemicals in Snowberry Creek and Bigfork River. Someone had to put pressure on Einhorn to ensure that everything was properly cleaned up. Payouts would take time, and someone had to manage that as well.

She figured there was nobody better suited to be that someone than her.

"Speaking of indefinitely," Logan said, "I've been thinking about staying here, too."

"Staying?" The idea was a shock and a thrill rolled into one. So far, he was using up his vacation days, which they both knew would run out sooner or later. She'd chosen not to stress out about it and simply enjoy whatever time they had together. "But what about your job and your family. You're talking about a life-altering decision."

"Summer, you've already altered my life. In all the best ways. Sure, we could do this long-distance, but I don't want to, and I don't think you do either."

She didn't. Going to bed every night with Logan, making love to him, waking up in his arms, holding him, kissing him, talking about everything face-to-face. That was what she wanted most. To deepen their close connection.

"Why should we put ourselves through that torture, when there's no need," he said. "I can do law enforcement anywhere. Chance even told me if I ever wanted a job with IPS, then I'd have one. I've been ready for a major change for a while. My place isn't on the Shooting Star-Longhorn Ranch. My home is here, with you."

Her heart was doing somersaults. But she didn't want him to regret such a big choice. "Are you sure? There's no rush to decide."

He smiled, the flash of his dimples tempting her to lean across the table and kiss him. "Now you sound like me after you told me you were ready to make love."

She remembered the conversation, outside, in the bright light of day, holding hands. Not in the heat of the moment. He'd been such a gentleman, wanting to ensure she didn't have any regrets.

But she had been certain.

Logan had lit candles, taken his time, drawing out her pleasure. The experience had been tender and passionate and better than any fantasy.

How could she ever regret making love to such an incredible man who made her feel desired and so special?

"Summer, we have something good. Great. This feels right. You and me. I've got a good chunk of money saved. I was thinking we could buy a house together. Make it ours."

Stunned, she gaped at him. "That's serious."

"I'm serious. About you. About a future together. I want to put down roots with you. Not in Cutthroat Creek. I was thinking Bitterroot Falls," he said, drawing a smile to her face. "I want to take the next step. But we don't have to if you want to take things slow. I can rent my own place. Everything has been fast and furious for us. I don't want you to be overwhelmed. That's why I've been waiting to bring it up."

The warm, intense look in his eyes made her chest fill with joy and nerves, all at once. "It has been fast, but I love you, Logan."

He reached over and stroked her cheek. "I love you, too." Leaning across the table, he cupped the back of her head and kissed her. "Does that mean—"

She cut him off with another kiss. "It means I'm ready. For us to take the next step." They were already living together. Quite happily. Effortlessly even in tight quarters. "I don't need slow when it feels right and it does to me, too."

"I want everything with you, Summer Stratton."

Smiling, she felt the same. Loving and supporting each other, building a life together, she was certain their future would be nothing short of amazing.

* * * * *